It gets Greater Later

Yvonne Bridges

Bridges II Paradise
P.O. Box 67
Kirkwood, De 19708-0067

www.bridges2paradise.com

Cover Design/Graphics:
Kevin Carr
newmedia2009@gmail.com

Book cover Model:
Iola Bridges
bridges2paradise@aol.com

Editor:
Joanne Howard
jo.howard@rcn.com

Typesetting:
Shawna A. Grundy
sag@shawnagrundy.com

ISBN# 0-9788146-1-4

Mr. William
Thanks for the
Support
Yvonne Bridges

It gets Greater Later

Acknowledgements

1 Corinthians 2:9:

"Eye has not seen, nor ear heard; nor have entered into the heart of man the things which God has prepared for those who love Him."

First and foremost, I have to give all praises to my Lord and Savior Jesus Christ. Without you, I would have never discovered me. I thank you daily for saving a wretch like me. No one or no love is greater.

A special thank you to my husband and children—Their constant support and understanding of my work promote inspiration to catapult me forward. There are not enough words to express my love. Again I thank God for giving me each and every one of you.

My wonderful mother and siblings—I wouldn't trade you guys for anything in the world. You all are so greatly appreciated.

My editor—Thank you again for understanding my style and I appreciate your hard work.

To my beautiful niece, Iola Bridges—Thanks for posing for my book cover. Remember what you make happen for others God will make happen for you. Hold on to all of your dreams, they will soon come to past.

For my many host of friends, extended family members, and everyone who I might be forgetting…Remember, I still love all of you and the support that you all showed will last a life time.

My growing audience and dedicated readers, *Everybody*

Gets Tired, but you have not; therefore, I truly wish to thank you for the love, support and the great responses that I received. This is what keeps me writing.

To TBN: thanks for your network and all of the inspiring Pastors that you air.

To Mr. Steve Harvey: thanks for your morning inspiration.

This book is dedicated
to
Mrs. Deborah Cannon

This one is for you!

Prologue

It was a cold and rainy day and drops were pound-ing against the broken window as my brother, Kevin and I played. My little mind was always faster than my body. I was always thinking and wondering about life. If my memory serves me correctly, I had to be at least five years old during this particular period in time. We all have a day in life that we will always remember. This is my day. It is the first time in my brief life that I've ever seen men dressed so well, especially white men. Yeah…these were white men with attitudes; tall and well dressed. They were so arrogant. They felt no need to acknowledge my brother and me. Umm…They didn't acknowledge my father either except to give him his package. There were no greetings or salutations; not even a slight smile. Even so, the taller of the two always had some small token of "gratitude for sharing your momma" with us. It was usually in the form of a toy; usually given to us before taking my momma into the bedroom. At least, he was nicer than the other men that came around. Unfortunately, his niceness would be short lived, especially this day.

When momma had visitors, Kevin and I would look out the window and pretend we didn't hear any kind of noises coming from the bedroom. She would make all kinds of funny noises. Daddy sat stoically with his eyes fixed on the television pretending he did not hear or see anything. When the men were finished doing their business with momma, daddy generally joined them in a smoke or two. This particular day was different. Today, the two men came as usual. The taller of the two was always very nice to my brother and me. He would not say much but there was something gentle in his facial expression. Most importantly, he would always have a toy for us. This day we received Candy Land and Operations. Sometimes, I got the impression that he felt sorry for us. The other man was detached. He came to handle business and that was all. His eyes would always peruse the environment. But, there was something strange about his demeanor this day. There was something strange going on in his eyes. His demeanor was uneasy. It was the first time that I was scared. Scared for me; my brother and mother. His attitude possessed a hint of anger. He made his way through the dirty clothes, the trash thrown about and grabbed my momma by her hair. Kevin and I ran over to help her, but my daddy stopped us. Shook by what we just witnessed and tears streaming down our face, we hugged our father as we waited to see what would happen next.

"Hey man why so rough! We can save this action for the bedroom. Get a grip, respect. My kids are just in the other room," momma shouted as she was continuously pulled into the room.

"Shut the hell up and get in here. You just couldn't keep your big mouth shut, huh? You dumb ass." The man yelled all sorts of obscenities as he continued to throw momma around the room. Momma possessed a confused, gazed look at the tall white man. One smack after another landed against my momma's frail body. She almost looked like a poor black, Raggedy Anne doll as she finally landed in a resting spot on the floor. Kevin and I remained steadfastly by dad's side waiting patiently for him to intervene on momma's behalf. When I think back on that moment, dad had as much fear in him as we did.

Momma, half dazed, attempted to get control of the situation as she seductively undresses while crawling on the floor. Screams and shouts radiated the air. I don't know who I felt sorrier for—my poor, defenseless momma or my scared, half-witted father. Suddenly, daddy decided to be a man and make a move which quickly was diverted by the other white man. He threw my daddy a white plastic bag with powder in it. We knew from that point, daddy would be no good at protecting or at least, trying to save poor momma. Daddy scrambled for the bag while my momma was fighting for her life. It is at this point that I lose track of time. The last audio memory of that night was the loud thunderous voice stating, "I told you to keep them a secret." The last visual memory of my momma was lying motionlessly under a white sheet and my daddy being hauled away in handcuffs. My brother and I zombie-like bodies sat stiffly in the back of the police car scared to death and unable to make sense of what had just taken place.

1

"Rise and shine idiots. It's time for school." The voice I came to regret bellows.

"I can't stand that ugly, horse face wench." Before I could finish my sentence, Frankie interrupts me and whispers, "Who? The lady who feeds us and clothes us!"

"Frankie shut up! Why is it that you never have anything bad to say about her? She's mean as hell and you know she only keep us here for the money."

"Well…I look at it this way, the last three homes we were in gave us very little for the money. We were beaten, battered, molested and starved most of the time. So…the way I see it, this is like living in Beverly Hills."

"You are either crazy or just downright stupid. Or, maybe…and I really hate saying this, but just maybe, you have a point. It could be worse. At least I know that we're no…you're sleeping well at night and that should be enough for me."

"Kyla…what about you? You are always worrying about me. How are you doing in school?"

"I told you, and I don't know why I continue to repeat myself. I go to school just so I won't go to jail and so I won't have to hear the wench's mouth."

"I heard that," hollered Ms. Greir. "You two need to be concerned about school so… I suggest that you get a move on before ya'll are late for school."

"Kyla, I'm starting to feel that urge again."

"Urge? Come on…for what Frankie?"

"I don't know. Sometimes, I just feel the urge or the need to get high."

"Well, keep in mind the end result which is not good. You don't have too many options as far as I can see. Realistically, you only have one. If you drop dirty urine, you'll go to the juvenile detention center; no visitors, no money and you'll probably get caught up in your old activities again. As of next week, you will have a year clean. Let's not blow it."

"It's amazing! You have your own problems but you know how to remember the things that are important to me. How is that?"

"Boy, please! Right now, you are all I have and for that reason, I remember everything about you. Umm… you know, since the state separated my brother and me, it's been a tough road. In a way, you fill the void in my life that was left there."

"I told you that God brings people together for a reason. Maybe, just maybe, God realized that we both needed someone."

"God! There you go again talking that bull! You know I have my issue with your God. Anyways, it's getting late and we need to get a move on, Remember I love you and stay clean."

"I'll do that but you need to remember that God loves all of us and regardless of our trials, it gets greater later." As we headed out of the door, Frankie and I exchanged hugs and laughter. He was the only thing I had in my life that was real. Frankie is a mixture of Italian and Spanish. He is very nice looking. In fact, he's so handsome that he gets mistaken for a girl. We've been in the same foster care for almost eight years now. Our social worker understood the importance of keeping us together. If we're not kept together most likely we'll run away until we find each other.

Frankie was placed in the system because he was abused by his father. I don't know how true it is and I only have his word to go on, but he tells me that his father would beat him because he looked like a girl. He was called all sorts of names and his life was made a living hell. The daily name calling was so common that poor Frankie began to believe that his name was *sissy* or *faggot* for the first ten years of his life. Frankie's mother was no help at all in protecting her son. She is an extremely religious person and believes in sticking by her man 'until death do them part'. Until the state stepped in, poor Frankie had no one to protect him from the abuse of his father. After hearing his story and the abuse that he endured, it only solidifies my disbelief in God and the church. These 'holier than thou' individuals irritate me to no end. These people are so religious that they totally forget about their earthly purpose.

Once the state took control of Frankie, he was shuffled from one foster home to another. His security or sense of family was derived from the kids on the street. The street, the kids, and all of the junk of life became part of Frankie. By the time he was thirteen, he tried every street drug that was accessible. His drug-induced stupor engaged him in all different types of sexual relationships to support his habit. He did not engage in petty crimes to support his addiction. He used what God gave him—good looks. Poor Frankie! Because of his sexual promiscuity, especially with men, he believes that he is gay. The lost soul has never had a woman. I have grown to be his voice of reasoning. Daily, I have to remind him that he's only sixteen and he doesn't know what he is. As he allows God to be the voice of reasoning for him; he must allow time to decide his sexuality.

Frankie and I made a promise to each other. I promised him that I would stop street hustling and scamming people only if he would stop getting high and engaging in homosexual acts. I also attend weekly meetings with him and he goes to church every Sunday. With all that he has endured, he still maintains a belief in God. I guess his religious beliefs are embedded in him since his mother dragged him to church seven nights a week. This is where we differ. I find it hard to believe in God. I often question how God can exist witnessing the suffering that so many on earth must endure. My summation is that we are living in a screwed up world. I let Frankie have his faith; it keeps him focus and he prays for me all the time. So, if there is a God, then He knows my pain here on earth.

Frankie and I have our dreams. We have plans of owning our own business one day. We are uncertain of the nature of that business, but it will be ours. As far as I am concerned, he is the youngest, wisest person that I know. I believe he's been here before. As mean and hateful as his father has been to him, he still has forgiveness in his heart for this man. Frankie believes that if we can't forgive people then we must ask ourselves why we expect God to forgive us. I love his positive attitude. He even believes that one day we are going to find a family that genuinely loves us; we are going to be happy and have a stable home. I guess I'm just pessimistic at times, because I can't see that far. I'm seventeen years old and time is slipping on by. The day I turn eighteen is the day of freedom. Freedom from the homes, schools, and the state. I can only imagine what my life will be like. One thing for sure, it has to be better than it's been.

Since that horrible night, my life has been a living hell. All I know is the streets and how to survive in them. Since the age of ten, I have been a known thief. If it wasn't nailed down, I would steal it. And, if I got caught, so be it. The one thing I am sure of is that I never did drugs a day in my life. The only time that I have been prescribed prescription meds was during labor. At the age of sixteen, I had given birth to my daughter, Sky. Sadly, her name is the only thing I have been able to give her. Early in her young life, I would make a mistake and custody would be given to her father, Taron. He is a very nice, hard working man with a set of values. We met during one of my street hustles. I had stolen a PlayStation system and was attempting to sell it. Being the nice guy, he, without hesitation, offered me $150.00 and told me to give the game to a kid that needed some happiness in his life. At that moment, I was impressed by his kind and unselfish manner.

He was uncertain of my age at the time of our encounter. Amazingly, my looks have always been deceiving. Some days I would look a bit older and then other days, I looked my age. Regardless, I associated the confusion in my age to the moment in time, environment; whatever worked. Since I was rather young when my brother and I were separated from my people, I don't know much about my roots. All I can remember is that their skin tones were darker than mines. In essence, I am what Negroes label "passing." I blended with blacks, whites, and Hispanics. Inquisitively Taron asked, "What is a pretty girl like yourself doing out here hustling? You should be on somebody's runway or maybe in a magazine instead of this cold dark street trying to sell electronics. Especially stolen electronics!"

"Why don't you just mind your business? You know nothing about me or my dealings."

"Sorry if I offended you. Really…I did not mean any harm." He politely introduced himself and asked if I wanted to get something to eat. I agreed. He became a means to an end that day. I wasn't interested in him, but he offered me better comfort than I'd been having. For one night, I did not have to accept the living conditions of the shabby hotel. I loved Frankie but his antics were displacing us over and over again.

It seemed as though Frankie and I were always being relocated from one foster home to the next. With the constant relocation, we became emotionally detached from the situation. Our goal was to remain together. This time, the state wanted to separate us. Frankie's behavior was more than the foster parents wanted to manage. He was constantly breaking curfew, coming in high, and being disrespectful. The other foster kids were always jealous of us. They would lock us out so we could miss our curfew. But worst than that, they would steal money from our foster parents and frame either Frankie or I. I guess our case worker felt that we may do better apart; or, she had had enough of our foolishness. In any event, while we were awaiting placement, Frankie and I decided to skip. The shabby hotel became our home away from home for a few days, at least until the system caught up with us. We had learned to be resourceful; fortunately for the two of us, we always managed to keep money.

Regardless of how Frankie was mistreated by the other kids in the home, he never wanted to extract revenge. He would always keep his cool. I found myself becoming more annoyed at his nonchalant, pacifist attitude. I did not want cool; I wanted a reaction. I did not want a punk behavior; I wanted a masculine behavior. "Stand up to their bull. Fight back," I would scream at him. It did not make any difference. He would always say, "I'm just visiting here, God has bigger plans for my life." Then he would further elaborate that punkish statement with, "Although fate presents the circumstances, how you react depends on your character." Now who could argue with that? Well, this particular night, our house parent had had enough of Frankie's disrespect and disregards for the rules. She grabbed Frankie and started smacking him in the face and head. Mr. "God has greater plans" wasn't even trying to fight back. This dumb-ass woman must have lost all common sense. At one point, she began to choke Frankie. He was turning blue. At this point, I had had enough. Frankie could sit there and take that beating but I did not have to watch. I grabbed the nearest instrument which happened to be a broom and went directly upside her head. When she hit the floor, I grabbed Frankie and we ran out of the door.

"Thanks again. It seems as though you are always saving me from some sort of ugly fate."

"Frankie, I need for you to tell me something. You talk so much bull and refuse to cover your ass. Why? Where was God when that crazy woman was beating the crap out of you? You or your God didn't even try to stop her from choking your ass."

"The bible says, if someone strikes you, you should turn and give them the other cheek."

"So…that is what the bible says. Well…um…the next time you decide to talk and run off at the mouth or offend someone, throw in a bible verse or two. I bet you one thing for sure; they will beat the crap out of your bible-quoting ass. I guess you have some place for us to stay, uh! If not, you should know right now that I only have a couple hundred dollars. This will only last us a week or two."

"Call big Rob, he'll help us out."

"Us, you don't have to sleep with his fat ass just to get money. I feel like you're pimping me sometimes man."

"Thomas Fuller is quoted as stating, no man can be happy without a friend, nor be sure of his friend until he is unhappy."

"Frankie don't start with the quotation bull, why won't you quote where were going to sleep tonight."

"It's all in God's plan." I flagged Frankie and walked away. Myra knew the routine. She would gather me and Frankie's personal items and wait for us to call her. She would sneak out of the house and bring them to us. Myra was a foster child too, but she was a real good kid. She had graduated from high school and received a full scholarship to college. She was real good people. She was so good that our foster mother permitted her to remain even beyond the age of emancipation and there was no state money for her. She had a true liking for Frankie. She enjoyed his company and his many unfortunate mishaps.

This one particular time one of Frankie's religious proverbs held some truth. This is when I met Sky's father, Taron. Frankie swears that Taron was an answer to a prayer. He became our angel that night. The condition of me having dinner with him was predicated on Frankie accompanying us. He agreed and we had us a great meal in a fancy restaurant. Taron was blown away by Frankie. He was trying to hold his laugh in all night. I said, "It's okay to laugh at him, he's a character and sometimes he's in a world all of its own. It was both Frankie and mines first time in a four star restaurant. Frankie was a real character; one would have thought by his behavior that he was a true connoisseur. Taron let Frankie do all of the ordering and the sampling. Frankie is gifted and rather talented. He's an advocate reader and fluently speaks Spanish and Italian. He'll read anything and everything. I think if properly tested, he may just be labeled a genius or something. Life has taught him a lot during his brief tour. There wasn't a shy bone in his body. I guess in a way, his free spiritedness is truly why I love him so. While Frankie was entertaining both the waiter and busboy, I was enjoying Taron.

As Taron and I got to know each other better, we began to exchange personal information. Upon learning of his age, I was too embarrassed to tell him my real age, so I lied. I told him that I was eighteen years old. "Well I'm usually attracted to women my age or older than me. I don't know what it is about you, but I am finding you to be extremely attractive." I'm sitting there thinking to myself, "Umm…I know what you're attracted to…this perfectly shaped body and this equally gorgeous face. Oh…I don't want anyone to think that I am conceited, but I know my assets and if the need arises, I will use them." Sometimes I feel like my looks are a curse and a blessing. I use my outer parts more than my inner parts.

Generally, I used my looks to manipulate any situation; especially involving a guy. Frankie always says, "Girl, you just don't understand the blessings that God has laid upon you." Every now and then, I allowed my intelligence to surface.

Frankie could be so pig-headed. He knew how infuriating all that God talk made me, but he would continue to rattle off at the mouth. My only response would be beauty and brains are all God has to offer me. I am homeless. I have no family. And, last but not least, I am angry. And… you are ranting that I am blessed.

"God shows mercy to who He wants to." Usually, I would give into such discussions because with Frankie, you cannot win against him and his God. I knew that I was smart. At the age of thirteen, I took the SAT just to prove to Frankie that the test is not as challenging as it seems. Even to my astonishment, I was twenty points away from a perfect score. After that test, Frankie finally conceded that I did possess some level of intelligence other than hustling.

After meeting Taron, our lives turned for the better. Taron had recently purchased a duplex and was in the process of rehabilitating the structure. He offered both Frankie and I a place to stay; at least until we could figure out our next move. Taron provided almost all of our necessities. He did have a few requests; Frankie must continue with his education and I must end my hustling career. Quietly, I laughed to myself; if only he knew my true age. Anyways, Frankie did not have a problem with finishing his education; I had a problem with shutting down my hustle. Secretively, I decided to drop out of school. I had concluded that a high school education was not my cup of tea; personally, I felt I was smarter than most of the educators anyways. I did know that if Taron had known my real age things would have been completely different. More than likely, he would have sent us both packing. I managed to acquire my GED that same year. As far as the two of us were concerned, things were going well for us. I was rather surprised that the Department of Human Services was not looking for the two of us.

Taron became part of our family or we became part of his; either way, the three of us were happy, at least in the beginning. He treated us very well. As time passed, I began to develop feelings for him; some would think that at one point I loved him. The relationship did bother me. This was a good man. He was good to me. He sincerely cared about my welfare. But…Something deep down inside just kept eating at me. Maybe I was just pessimistic; I knew or felt that eventually all good things would come to an end. I just kept wondering about the end. Taron had real family. He had two parents. He had siblings. He had values and dreams. He knew what he wanted and what it would take for him to be successful. He was unlike Frankie and I; we just went with the flow. We developed a family routine. We would have dinner together; talk about our day; play a game of Scrabble. The three of us got along well together. After six months of living in heavenly bliss, the dark cloud descended upon us. I was pregnant. I did not know what to feel, but Taron was ecstatic. Even poor mixed-up Frankie was happy. Personally, I could only feel jealous. Jealous of a life growing inside of me.

Taron re-designed the layout of the duplex. The baby, he, and I would reside on the second level; Frankie's residency is the third level. The first floor was still leasable and an artsy couple signed a year's lease agreement. Taron and I started hanging out a lot. I stopped hustling and found a job as a telemarketer. I was good at hustling so this was a legitimate way for me to swindle people. Frankie befriended the couple from the first floor. They were spending many hours together. Moore was an art major and his wife Joanie was a night club singer. Frankie, being the great social politician, was able to convince the couple that he was well versed in the fields of art and music. So, they showed Frankie a lot of new things; some he did not need.

Frankie's grades were excellent. Taron and I didn't have any problems with his association with the couple until the day we noticed him drinking with them. This was a problem because first, he was under age. They being the adult should have been more conscientious of this fact. Then, he started pill popping with them. I was furious. I smacked Frankie. He was so high he didn't even know what had hit him. I physically whipped Joanie's ass, pregnant and all. Fortunately, this was a violation of the lease agreement. Taron terminated the lease and made them vacate the apartment immediately. This was just a small obstacle to Frankie. He continued to socialize with them. Where ever they had relocated to, Frankie spent many nights with them. Plenty of nights he didn't come home and I would beat the pavements looking for him. This situation interfered with my relationship with Taron. He became annoyed with my concern over Frankie.

"Kyla, I know that you love Frankie, but you have to think and show concern about the life that you're carrying." I knew he was right. But, he had to understand the relationship between Frankie and I; he was my family. He and I had been through so much together. I just could not abandon him.

One night while Taron and I were trying to rest, the police came to the apartment looking for Frankie. I became terrified.

"Excuse me officer, why are you looking for him?"

"He stole a car that belongs to a couple that he was staying with."

Taron interrupted, "Well…no officer we hadn't seen him, but we will call you if he comes here." The officer gave us a nod and went on his way.

I said, "What the hell do you mean we will call them?

I am not turning him in. They will put him in the juvenile detention center."

"That's probably what he needs, Kyla. You are not his mother. You need to worry about your own life and that of our child's." That was it. I got up; drove around all night until I found Frankie. He was standing under a bridge trying to solicit. He looked so bad. He looked as if he didn't shower in days. A Mercedes Benz pulled up to Frankie and called him over to the car. I immediately jumped between them. I threw Frankie in my car and we drove to the nearest hotel. I ordered food for him and I gave him a shower. His young addicted body was weak and his words were sluggish. He did not recognize me, but he knew I was there. He was so wasted. He kept saying, "Moore told me that he loved me, he said he was leaving Joannie for me." I couldn't believe this bastard was using him. Frankie is a boy. Sometimes I felt as if he did not want to grow up. What was I to do? My hands were tied. If I were to go to the police, Frankie would be the one to pay. Back to the detention center he would go. Possibly, back to foster care. My only recourse was Taron. He loved me and I know he had love for Frankie. I made that call and as expected, Taron told me to bring him home.

Tomorrow was a new day. The next morning, Frankie and I got up and ate breakfast. I washed Frankie's clothes while he was sleeping. I was too embarrassed to ask him what happened between him and Moore. I made him promise to stay away from him and Joanie. He also made other promises—to return to school and drug counseling. Frankie said, "My girl; always around when I need her. You are a true friend. Even if I make a fool of myself, you believe it isn't forever."

"Thanks Frankie. You know that I love you, and like

you always rant, "You know that it gets greater later."

2

Frankie began to put a strain on my relationship with Taron. Any day I was scheduled to give birth; yet, I was constantly babysitting Frankie instead of preparing for my delivery. I delivered Sky on a Friday. Frankie named her. He said he named her that because the sky was the limit to her success. Taron and I agreed on the name. Sky was everything to Taron and me. Surprisingly, I never thought that I could love someone so much. That initial jealousy had been replaced by unconditional love. We, both, were so in love with her. Taron was the perfect father. Whenever he heard her make a sound, he would run to her. I thought the child wasn't going to be able to use her vocal cords. He did not want her crying. Unwavering attention was bestowed upon her. Taron being the man with values wanted to make our arrangement legitimate. Immediately, after Frankie's graduation celebration, he popped the question. I couldn't believe it. What was I to do as a mother and a wife? I was trying to get Frankie squared away for college. Life became overwhelming. I was afraid of such pressure. I explained to Taron how much I loved him and how much I appreciated him and everything he has done, but I think it would be a good idea if we slowed things down. Taron was patient and understanding. By the look in his eyes, I could see the hurt. He kissed me and Sky then nodded his head in agreement. There was so much he did not know about me. I still had not confessed my true age. Lies were the barrier that kept me from being free. After Frankie's graduation, skeptically, we agreed to permit him to hang out in Atlantic City. Even if we would have refused, I don't know if that would have kept Frankie from going. He could be stubborn and he was adamant about going. Anyways, Taron and I could have used a break. That weekend was a great weekend.

We took Sky to the zoo. She laughed at the giraffes and was terrified of the snakes. Marriage was still on the forefront of Taron's mind. Every opportunity, he would drop little hints about me becoming his wife. I would just give him a friendly smile and say, "soon baby, real soon." Our great weekend was not destined to last forever, the very next morning we received a call stating that Frankie had gotten into trouble. The officer couldn't explain it over the telephone and someone needed to come to Atlantic City. This was not a good thing. Sky was not feeling well. I instructed Taron to stay home and attend to her while I go and find out what was going on with Frankie. I arrived at the Atlantic City Police Station as fast as I could. The officer drove me to the nearest hospital and there laid Frankie handcuffed to a bed. A car had hit him. The police was holding him because he was a witness in a casino robbery. While the officer was trying to explain what happened, Frankie interrupted, "Kyla that's not what happened. My friends and I were having a good time and we got caught in the cross fire of a shoot out. I didn't see anyone rob anything."

The officer interrupted Frankie, "How do you know what you saw, you were so high, I'm surprised you remember anything. Excuse me miss, as I was saying, we are willing to let him out on $50,000.00 bail. Of course, you would only have to pay $5,000.00, that's ten percent of the bail."

"Officer, I don't have that kind of money on me."

Well you'll have to get it by 8:00am tomorrow morning or he will be shipped to the prison until a court date is set."

I looked at Frankie and sympathetically stated, "What happened? There must be more to it. If you are only a witness, why the bail? I don't know what to believe. But, I'm here. I'll do what I can."

"Okay officer, I'll see what I can do." I couldn't dare get the nerve up to ask Taron. He's a good man; a good provider. Since the birth of Sky, I have not wanted for anything. All I knew was that I couldn't leave Frankie in prison. They will eat him alive in there. I had to think and I had to think fast. My only alternative was a hustle. God, I am right back at the beginning; where I don't want to be. I went to the mall and purchased a nice sexy dress and a pair of pumps. I washed in the ladies room then changed my clothes. For some reason, I've always attracted older white men. I have an eye for the ones with the money, so it was time to go to work. I sat at the black jack table drinking apple martinis and pretending to be spending a lot of money and my high roller victim was sitting right next to me. He was half drunk. He was loaded with chips and alcohol.

"Hey beautiful, how much are you spending?"

I ignored him the first time. He repeated himself, but this time he passed me a drink along with the sorry line. "I'm just out to have a little fun tonight."

"Well it seems like we have something in common.

I'm trying to have some fun too." He ordered drink after drink and he was winning. I asked, "Are you by yourself? If so, you do not need anything else to drink. Maybe… You need just beautiful company. Why don't you let me escort you to your room?"

"You most certainly can." I helped the man up and showed him to his room. As soon as we got there, he started kissing on me. "Hey how about if you take a shower first, I'll be waiting for you when you get out." He stumbled to the bathroom, started the shower and proceeded to wash. I knew after giving him a shower and a massage, that he would go straight to sleep and that he did. I took his voucher to cash in his chips and I headed towards the pay out counter. I grabbed a payout slip for seven thousand dollars. The next day I bailed Frankie out. Frankie has never been this terrified before. He begged me to get him out of Philadelphia.

"Why Frankie? What can be that bad that you can't be seen in Philadelphia?"

"I did see something that I should have not seen and I'm scared. I don't want to tell you because you would be at risk too."

"Frankie, I thought you promised me that you were not going to get high."

"I didn't do any drugs; I was just drinking."

"Frankie…you have an addictive personality; you shouldn't drink or do any substance that leads to intoxication."

"Well Ms. Perfect, don't let me seem ungrateful for your help. Should I assume that Taron loaned you the money to help me out? Umm…I see your dress in the back of the car. If your man didn't give you the money, I'm sure that black dress was not just decorations! How did you get the money to get me out"? Jesus said, "Let thee without sin cast the first stone! So…with that being said…apparently, you still have your game too!"

"If I were you, I would be careful with what I have to say. You ungrateful…Just watch your mouth Frankie. I'm not in the mood for your bull. I'm putting my life on hold to babysit your ass, so please don't make matters worse. Better yet, don't let me regret my dumb decision to help you!"

Frankie turned beet red. He started hollering, "Go ahead with your new so called clean life and your new family. You know that you are all that I have; I knew you would kick me to the curb when you had that baby." Frankie jumped out of the moving car. I couldn't believe it. There were no cars in back of us so he was safe. I saw him get up and limp away. I followed him for few blocks and then he started running. "Frankie, please get back in the car." He ignored me and kept on running. "Frankie please…please just get back in the car. I am tired."

Frankie dashed into the woods and needless to say that was the last time I saw or heard from him. I arrived home and Taron and Sky was sitting up waiting for me. Taron verbally attacked me as soon as I walked through the door. "What the hell is wrong with you? Are you going to let that little junkie destroy your family? Destroy you? Destroy us? Don't even answer! The police was here looking for you. How could you be so selfish?"

"For me?"

"Yeah…I didn't stutter. Apparently you haven't seen the morning news. The old man that you tricked or robbed or whatever the hell you did was an undercover detective looking for whores to arrest. I guess he found one!"

"Are you calling me a whore?"

"If the shoes fit, wear them." In the middle of the argument, sirens and red lights began flashing throughout the apartment. I was terrified. "Kyla, what do you want me to do? I love you, but I do not want to raise Sky this way."

"Please help me…this last time. I promise you… Taron, please just let me hide somewhere and I'll leave tomorrow. I am giving you my word. I will leave and you will not have to hear from me again. I promise you I won't keep causing you pain." Taron pulled me by my arm and hid me in a closet that he was reconstructing. I heard Sky hollering and Taron trying to convince the police that I wasn't there. They searched each room and every entrance thoroughly. This was the night of living hell. What else could possible go wrong? I didn't know what to do or what to think. Was Frankie okay? Did Taron still love me? Is he going to take Sky away from me? I needed answers. I wanted to believe that this entire day was just a nightmare; tomorrow will be just like yesterday and the day before. All I knew was if there was a God, where was he now because I needed for this nightmare to be over. I closed my tired eyes and for the first time, I prayed for a better tomorrow. A different tomorrow. I just needed to rest and think.

Morning came quickly. When I opened my eyes, I woke to find four packed suit cases, three thousand dollars, a disappointed man and a beautiful crying baby. It wasn't getting better nor was it getting greater.

3

I awoke in a cold sweat only to realize that my life was not a dream. It was real. My newly found family was gone and so was my happiness. I felt emptiness deep inside. I missed my little girl. It has been three years since I've seen her. I know she's beautiful and running her daddy wild. I think of Frankie at least a hundred times a day. It is difficult for me to believe that he would abandon me. I should be annoyed, angry, and resentful but I love him and I just wanted to reassure him. I have checked every drug house; all of his weird friends but no one heard from him. I guess it's just me against this cold, cold world. I am certain that I can take care of myself whether I want to or not. Now I can be who I want to be. No restraints. I am finally free. I don't have that extra baggage any longer. If Frankie thinks that he can live without me, I damn sure can live without him.

First things first, I must get out of this dump. I thought the hood in Philly was bad, but Chester is worse. This town is too small; everybody knows everybody's business. I just don't have time for the extra bull. From all of the misfortune, I teamed up with some other players that I knew from Philly. Since the unpleasant incident with Frankie, I have major trust issues. My comfort level is me working alone.

Sooner or later my luck would come to an end. As my luck goes, it came sooner. I should have taken a look out person with me when I did my last job; unfortunately, I was trying to get a quick beat, but it lead me to the worst eighteen months of my life. One night I waited all night for what I thought was a sweet setup. I decided to venture to an AMC movie theater in a local suburb. I parked and observed. I was scouting for my perfect victim. Wealthy people have a tendency to be complacent with their surroundings. Suddenly, I eyed the perfect couple getting out of what looked to be a brand new Lexus. I followed them as they approached the theater and made their purchase. The female almost could pass for a model. She was stylishly dressed. Accompanying her was a man, looking like he just stepped out of a GQ magazine. His features were similar to JFK, Jr. He was extremely handsome. Frankly speaking, they looked like the ideal couple. The woman appeared to handle the business. I watched as she paid for their food with a credit card. It wasn't just any credit card. It was an American Express; not just any American Express. Platinum. I knew that I had selected the perfect mark. I made sure I took a seat ten rows behind them. I waited for the both of them to get comfortable and for the movie to begin. The movie was dark and everyone was tentatively watching the flick, I decided to make my move. I crawled on the floor ten rows ahead of me and went into her pocket book. I took only three credit cards. I crawled back to my seat and waited for the perfect time to exit. Feeling sure of myself and the perfect score, I decided to exit the theater. Suddenly, a strong, tight grip was around my left arm. I tried to run but my feet were running on the air. When I looked over my shoulder, I noticed that it was the handsome guy from inside the movie theater.

"What the hell do you want?"

"I want what belongs to my wife."

"What the hell are you talking about? Get the hell off of me."

"You know damn well what I am talking about…give me my credit cards."

Immediately, I composed myself. I gathered my thoughts and with all of my strength, I kicked him in his manhood and ran. I was running as fast as I could. The faster I ran, the louder the sirens and the brighter the lights became. I had one more breath in me which would be my last breath of freedom. Before I realized my predicament, I was on someone's lawn with ten cops surrounding me. I couldn't believe it. All these damn police for a pick pocket scam. I knew it was over. A female officer patted me down, handcuffed me and threw me in the back of a police car. That was the rockiest ride I've ever been on. When I arrived at the station, someone would have thought that I robbed Commerce or Wachovia. There were news reporters and camera crew all over the place. I could not believe what I was seeing. My fingerprints were ran and my existing record did not help my situation any. This time, I knew I would be spending some time away. As soon as the doors slammed, I heard Frankie's little annoying voice quoting a famous saying, "Only some of us learn by other people's mistakes. The rest of us have to be the other people." His voice was so real. My mind was playing tricks on me. All of my wheeling and dealing finally caught up with me. I anticipated that this little capper would net me at least two years in Delaware County. Two years was the minimum. How could I have been so stupid and irresponsible?

Suddenly, I realized that I was alone. No one. Nobody. Just me; all alone. For one brief moment in my life, I did have someone. I had Taron. I had my daughter. I had screwed up big time. Even so, I knew I had to make that call and I dreaded doing it.

I was filled with embarrassment but several weeks passed, the courage came and I dialed. The phone rang two times and the sweetest baby toned voice answered, "Hello I'm Sky, who is this?" What was I to say? The word mommy was at the tip of my tongue, but what gave me the right to let that word roll off of my tongue. I stood still holding the phone for five more seconds and her little voice said it again, "Who is this? This is Sky." As my eyes began to swell, a tear fell and before I could answer, Taron's voice was emanating from the earpiece.

"Hello!"

"Hi…Taron this is Kyla." His voice changed instantly. He was shocked to hear from me. His voice was filled with excitement. My heart became very warm.

"Hello Kyla, how are you?"

"I'm fine but…I don't know if you are aware of my present situation, but…I'm in jail."

"I saw it on the news a couple of weeks ago. I was hoping you would call. Do you need anything?"

"Yes, I do. I can use whatever you can afford to send me. How's Sky? She sounds like an angel."

"She is an angel. She's beautiful and she looks exactly like you."

Before he could finish his sentence, I heard Sky screaming with excitement, "Hi Sherry!" Then Taron's voice whispered, "Hold on for a minute. Hi baby, you smell good." Taron always greeted me with kind words. At this point, I was emotionally handicapped. I was lost for words. What was I to say next? All kinds of thoughts were running through my head. Who is this Sherry? She has my family. I should be there. Taron should be loving me. I should be caring for my daughter. I should be raising her not some strange woman. She won't even know me when I get out. At that moment, I recalled Taron and me discussing my life choices during my pregnancy. He also clearly defined his position. He emphatically let me know that his child would not be raised on the street and associated with the prison system. If I go to jail, he would cut me off from our child. I can't blame him. I don't want to plant a seed like this in my baby's head. I don't want her to have ideas about being caged in. This was an inopportune time for me to relive my past. I should have known the price I would have to pay for being stupid; it's a heavy price.

"Hey Kyla, are you still there?"

"Yeah, where am I going?" As soon as I said that, a big sista walked up to me and without hesitation screams, "Times up, princess."

"Taron I have to go. Please give Sky a kiss for me."

"I sure will. You take care and feel free to call whenever you like."

"Thank y…" Before I could finish my words, this big Amazon chick snatched the phone from me and hung it up. I went crazy on her. I couldn't stop hitting her. I was beating her for all of my pains; old and new. My life was so messed up. I wasn't responsible for what was going to happen and to be honest, I didn't care. Her fellow prison workers had to peel me off of her. As usual, I would be paying for this mistake too. One ass whipping equals a week in the hole. That was a week in the pits of hell. I did not know it could get worst. It was dark, cold and smelled of urine. It has been a long time since I cried but here, I cried for the first three days, and then my spirit was completely broken. I tried to remember some of Frankie's encouraging words. The only words I could remember were "God will never leave me nor forsake me." I needed Frankie so much. I was mad at him for leaving me. For him, I was always there; my life has changed. I felt as though I was losing all sense of 'self;' all sense of being. It felt as if my soul was becoming disconnected from my body. That's when I knew I had to cry for help.

I tried several times to write Taron but I got no response. To add insult to injury, there was a report on the various news channels that an unidentified decomposed body, male, between the age of 18 and 21, possibly Hispanic was found in Camden, NJ. My entire body started to tremble. That was close to where Frankie jumped out of the car that day. I felt my body trembling and then, numbness swept over it. I had to do something, but what? I could pray. I did not know how to pray; even what to say. But, I had to do something. This was Frankie's God. He had to listen; even to me. On my knees I fell and the words flowed from my lips. This understanding God knew. Although I was mad at Frankie, I still loved him with all of my heart. He gave me inspiration. With him gone and me in jail, all I could hear was his little voice saying, "Hey Kyla, it gets greater later." If it is him, I know he's in heaven annoying the hell out of Jesus. He's probably telling God how to run things and the funny part is, God is probably listening and getting a kick out of him. Frankie always said, when he got to heaven he was going to explain to God why I didn't pray and why I didn't have faith. He was going to tell God that I was upset with him, because of the rough hand that He dealt me. He said he would convince God that I was a nice and smart person. That I loved and took care of him, so maybe God would have mercy on me. I guess God is not listening to Frankie, because life is still hell for me. If that unidentified body is Frankie, I wanted him to listen too. If he is listening, I wanted him to know that he wasn't doing a good job. You're not as smooth as you think you are. I wish you just convince God to take my life. I can't take any more hell on earth.

Why am I suffering like this? Frankie, I need for you to ask God to have mercy on me. Please. As these words reverberated in my mind so did thoughts of Frankie. These are similar words he, himself, would use. I must have been thinking out loud because, the girl in the cell next to me, shouted, "Shut the hell up, and stop blaming everyone else for you being here. You got what you got, for doing what you did, so deal with it."

"Who are you?"

"Just a woman trying to get some rest and tired of your whining. By the way, I have some words that you should remember…blessings come down when prayers go up."

"Again, I am asking….Who are you? You don't know anything about me."

"Umm… I may know more than you think."

She ignored me the rest of the night. I had nothing else to do but to cry myself to sleep. I was awaken by her voice, "Hey sis, if you're thinking about doing something stupid, like killing yourself, remember God gives life and it's his will for your life. In other words, don't be messing with his will."

Months went by and I was still alone. I had no visitors. As far as communication goes, Taron was sweet enough to send me pictures and money every month. I was extremely grateful for that. Sky is such a princess.

She's beautiful. I'm glad Taron made the decision he did with regards to her and visitation at the prison. I would not want the evil spirits of this place to be nowhere near her. My time was spent reading. Coincidentally, I found myself reading a lot of the same books that Frankie read. I guess this is my way to stay connected to him. My cell mate is pretty cool. She's very spiritual. I thought Frankie was deep. If Frankie was alive, they'll be running neck to neck with proverbs. Michelle just reinforced what Frankie was trying to instill in me. Every night she would pick a different topic. We discussed trust, forgiveness, abandonment, fear, faith, and almost every issue that I was dealing with in my life. Before each discussion, I had to say out loud, "*In all ways I must acknowledge him, and he shall direct my paths*." Proverbs 3:6.

I never asked Michelle what lead to her imprisonment, but rumor had it that she had killed her husband. She apparently was obsessed with him and had found him cheating one too many times. It's hard for me to understand how women or men for that matter could get themselves that worked up over another human being. How can someone love someone else so much that they loose themselves? It's like watching Lifetime TV and the women are being abused. Why don't they just leave? I guess that's one of the advantages of living from pillow to post; you're always disconnected from reality. I guess that same sista that committed murder or who was being abused would think that I'm an asshole for stealing credit cards. So, one thing that Frankie use to say that stuck with me like glue was, *"Judge not until you walk in someone else's shoes."* Michelle doesn't look like she can hurt a fly. Her man must have pushed her to the limit. I think she's cool but her biggest fault is that she pushes her values about God on other people. She reads to me a lot and that kills a lot of time. She has this pen pal that writes her uplifting letters. Each letter somehow reflects my life. The topic for tonight was *"The darkest hour is only 60 minutes long."* The author of these letters has a deep soul. Michelle constantly informs me that I'm not getting anything different because I'm not doing anything different. Her testimony is so powerful. She told me her story.

"The reason I can't go an hour without thinking about God is because when I was free, my life became tragic; when I stopped getting on my knees, I fell flat on my face. I was a bible school teacher, a mother and a wife before my prescription drug abuse took over my life. I was leaving bible school on a Wednesday night and I got mugged and rapped on the way home. I was horrified. I was in so much pain mentally, emotionally, and physically. I started taking Tylenol PM just to get me to sleep. Then I graduated to any narcotic that the doctor would prescribe. I blamed my sickness and sorrows on the Lord. How can He allow that to happen to me? I was under His submission, I was doing His work. I was paying tithes. I was volunteering every Sunday. I was giving offerings. I was praying and fasting. After I got raped, I stopped going to church. I stopped teaching bible school and eventually, I stopped praying. When it was all over, I was indebted to the devil. I was a soldier for him. I did everything and anything to ruin my life. So, when you look at this once beautiful, holy-filled woman and wonder why I'm always praising God, it's because when I stopped praising him I ended up here."

"Code Red, Code Red," came alarming through the intercom system. That's the emergency alert code. An inmate is probably attempting to commit suicide or something similar. This place is a nightmare. My cellmate can be a pain in the butt; however, she keeps me grounded and focused. She doesn't talk about her personal life that much. I'm surprised she shared part of her life's story with me. The only topic that she feels worth talking about is Jesus. As nights evolved into days and days into nights, my inner being was coming into place. I realized that I was not alone. Frankie words emerged into my mind, heart, and soul. God was with me; he did not forsake me. At that very moment, I dropped down to the floor and put my face on the floor. I begged God and cried out. I screamed so loud that I wanted it to reach Heaven. I pleaded for God to do some good things in my life. I challenged him. I cried, *"Dear God, please, please change my life. I want to live right and I want to be a mother to my daughter. I want a stable home and a stable life. Lord I've had it bad my entire life. I'm tired of hurting and pretending I'm okay. I'm tired of the numbness that I feel when it comes to love. I want to wake up one day and not be full of fear. I need you to replace it with faith. I want to trust people. Most importantly, I want to trust and believe in you. God if you are who Frankie and Michelle say you are, then show yourself to me."*

As my knees brushed against the coldness of the cement floor and tears fell from my eyes, I continued to pray. Father Frankie always said, *"If I believe and have faith that You are the only one who can perform the miracles that I need. My Heavenly Father today I surrender my life and will to you. I trust only in you. God I believe You are able to do it. Whatever it is that's missing or lacking in my life, I believe you can fix it. I'm stripped of every thing that I have and I'm coming to you bare and naked. Use me God to show your light. I'm opening up my heart and mind to You. I surrender."*

4

I'm so happy to be out of that hell hold. The half way house that I'm assigned seems to be pretty decent. It's clean but it's in a little hick town. Prior to my release, I was informed that I have to check in with my probation officer once a month. I'm going to do the right thing this time around. My probation officer has arranged a job for me at Starbucks. I don't drink coffee and I damn sure don't want to sell it. But, I have no space in my life to pick and choose right now. It is amazing the various types of characters that one meets serving coffee. One day while I was ringing up a customer, this very handsome face appeared in front of me. He was a very attractive white man. He looked very familiar but I couldn't place him. I think he felt an attraction between us, because I would always catch him staring at me. He came in the store at least twice a week. Sometimes he sat in the coffee shop for hours sipping on the same Latte. I thought to myself, who in the hell can drink this much coffee.

After weeks of watching me, he finally got up enough nerve to speak. "Hey beautiful, what's your name?"

I looked at him with the strangest look.

"You don't have to answer me, let me guess um… Kyla. It's on your earrings."

I stopped for a minute and starred at him, "Excuse me

is there something else that I may get you?"

"You."

I rolled my eyes and kept walking. He sipped on that same cup of coffee until the store was closing. As I was leaving the store, I noticed that he was following me. Probably, any other female would have been bothered by this action; I'm not any other female. I sat at the bus stop and he sat there with me. I continued to ignore him.

"I'm not following you and I'm not going to hurt you; as a matter of fact, I can help you."

"If you wanted to help me, you wouldn't have pressed charges. Therefore, the entire incarceration thing could have been avoided." While giving me a devilish seductive look, "My wife wanted to persue legal actions, I had something else in mind."

"And what might that be?"

"Let's grab a bite to eat and have a little chat." At first, I was a bit reluctant but my curiosity was getting the best of me. Not only that, God knows that I need help. He smelled so good and looked equally as good. My hormones were jumping. Why am I'm attracted to this man? I know that he's married and I know that he put my ass in jail. I must be losing it. I guess looking at women for almost two years of my life had made me desperate. "Where are we going?"

"Not far, it's a nice cozy restaurant up the street."

He ordered for the both of us. The food was delicious. It felt good being in the world again. I felt like I was on a date until he started with his scam. "Kyla how bad would you like to have custody of your daughter? It may be shared, but in any event, I can arrange custody."

I almost gagged. "How the hell do you know about my daughter?"

"I know everything about you. That was a nice scam you pulled at the movie theater. I have access to your life right now. I can get your probation cleared very quickly and I can make sure you get custody of your daughter."

"Who are you?"

"I'm a lawyer and I know a lot of influential people."

"If you know all of these influential people, then what do you want from me?"

"That's an open ended question." He gave me the cutest smile then he said, "I want you to steal. Only this time, it's my father's heart." I looked at him as if he was crazy. He laughed, "I want you to seduce my father."

I gagged on my wine. "You want me to do what!"

"My father is a wealthy bastard that lives in an exclusive retirement community. I want you to persuade him to give you access to his accounts and his investments, and then you'll give them to me."

"How do you know that your rich, white ass father is going to find me attractive?"

"Because he likes your kind."

"And what kind is that?"

"The kind that takes what she wants. He's attracted to sexy black girls with an uncaring attitude and besides we have the same taste." As the word taste was rolling off of his lips, I felt him caressing my thighs under the table. My mouth wanted to say stop, but my body was fighting it. John and I made out in a dark corner of an exclusive restaurant. He was so passionate. I was mad and happy at the same time. What the hell is wrong with me? I just broke a moral code of mine. I've never slept with a married man, and thought I never would. This was just the beginning of our affair. John used the excuse to set up our plan as a reason for us to meet every Friday.

We met at the same hotel for six months. He bought me gifts and helped me find an apartment. Basically, he was responsible for me getting back on my feet. Everything was moving along just fine; then after a passionate night of love making, he slipped and said the three painful words, "I love you."

"What did you just say?"

"I didn't stutter, I said I love you."

I immediately started to get dress. "There is no room for love. You don't love me. You love your wife. You need to remember her and just that. If you say it again, I'll tell her everything." I got dressed and left the hotel. Later, I called him and informed him that I wanted to end the affair. He begged me not to end it. "Look let's just get on with our plan, so I can go on with my life and get custody of Sky."

"Fine if that's the way you want it. I've arranged for you to begin work at Hockessin Hills Retirement Community. You need to be there at 7:00am sharp on Monday." I heard a loud bang in my ear. I assumed by the way he ended our conversation that he was unhappy about our situation. Unlike him, I knew what I wanted; what he wanted, in the end, was probably worth more than the lust he had for me.

5

When I walked into this beautiful building I almost lost my breath. Everything…Furniture and fixtures, from the floors to the ceilings were fabulous. The drapes looked as if they were all custom made and the oriental rugs were equally attractive. John made sure that I was aware that each person living at this well-established community is of millionaire status. This facility holds an Olympic-size swimming pool, a golf course, a stable of horses, and everything else that the rich and famous might desire. I noticed that the majority of the employees were white except for the line staff. My new position was in environmental services; in other words, housekeeping. After meeting with my supervisor and attending orientation, I was assigned a unit. This place is well maintained. It is difficult to imagine it getting dirty.

As I continued with my tour, I noticed my intended target—Judge John Chapman; evidently the son is Junior. Everyone calls him Judge. There must have been no love between father and son; especially since the son is arranging to steal from dear old dad. I cut through the court yard to get to the health care unit. With each step that I took, I could feel the stares coming from the pavilion. There sat Judge, an attracted old fellow with salt and pepper hair. He was joined by a very attracted black guy. The young black guy seemed to be caring for the old lady that was drawing at an easel. The two men were setting up for a game of Scrabble. I stopped to put a bag in a trash can and I heard them whispering from far away. The black guy muttered, "Underneath her street attitude and gaudy jewelry, she could be fine."

A strong, hardy voice said, "I see nothing but beauty. "She has a beautiful complexion and very exotic looking," said the older gentleman. I pretended that I was unaware of their lustful gazes and acted as if I wasn't listening. I could feel the older gentleman lusting as the older woman continued to draw. The two men continued their game of Scrabble both being competitive and daring.

"Hey what's your name?" I turned around very quickly with a look of shear amazement with a touch of innocent. "Are you speaking to me?"

Excuse me." I took the earphones out of my ear while he tried to lower his tone. "I'm sorry my name is Miles and this is Judge. What is your name miss?"

"Kyla."

Before I could answer, Judge said, "Kyla? How are you Kyla?"

I nodded my head towards him. "She has her name tattooed on her arm, her tongue pierced and she has her name looped in her earrings. Now that's what you call ghetto fabulous. I guess the HR Department is no longer strict with regards to who they hire," the so-called brother snorted.

"You are so judgmental Miles. Why are you so hard on her? What has she done to you? Everyone deserves a chance at earning a living."

"She needs more than a job; she needs a tab bit of polish. Girls like her simply annoy me. She's beautiful and ghetto. It hurts me to see my people walking around like the world owes them something. Her looks alone could have probably gotten her where she needs to be or what she wanted".

"Everyone cannot be as fortunate as you are. Has it ever occurred to you that this might be what she wants to do with her life? Remember…It is not doing the thing we like, but liking the thing we have to do that makes life happy. Have you forgotten from where you came? What if you had not been adopted into a well-to-do family, your fate may have been completely different? You could have traveled on her same road."

"At times I do wonder. As a matter of fact, I decided to search for my biological parents. I need to find my roots. Because I did not look like either parent, when I was young, my cousins would tease me and say that I look like the milkman's baby. They also use to call me half white boy because of my complexion and my hair texture. Now that I am older, I need to know from where I came. I need to know my roots."

Without any sense of courtesy or privacy, these two continued with their conversation. I couldn't help but to twitch my face to him. The nerve of this stuck up dude judging somebody. He's one of them high yellow people thinking that he's better than everybody. We are the same color and we both have the same texture of hair. So the hell what! He doesn't have a clue about my life. If I was dealt the hand that he was dealt, I would have a Master's degree or something of the sort. People kill me judging other people. I may not have the fancy college education but one thing for sure, I have life's education. I know how to survive. I had heard enough and I decided to move on.

During my break, I needed to re-direct my thoughts

from the earlier conversation. I'm glad that I have saved all of the letters that Michelle received from her pen pal. I feel like our souls are connected. I titled each of them according to my mood. I read these letters to constantly challenge myself. I feel like kicking this dude's ass but I must always remember that my actions always cause reactions.

Dear Michelle,

I'm incarcerated too, but I'm not behind bars nor do I get locked in at night. My mind and my thoughts are paralyzed. I am really afraid of change. I know if I can change my thoughts than I can change my life. I want to stop stealing and fornicating. I want to be an honest, law abiding citizen, but I'm covered with this curse. The thought of righteous living scares me. Every time I try to do right, wrong covers my rights, so I've come to realize that the power of life is in our tongue, so as of this day, I'm declaring to be free; not by my will but by God's will. I will start with my thoughts. From this day on, I will make a conscious decision to think positive.

Now that I gave myself some brain food, I can continue with my day.

I reconciled to the fact that my job was exactly that—a job. I enjoyed getting up and going to work every day. I contacted Taron and he agreed to let me see Sky although the courts didn't approve of it yet. I was so thankful for that. Taron had moved on. He and Sherry had gotten married and bought a beautiful home in the suburbs. At first, I was envious and then Frankie's words of wisdom immediately brought me back to reality. "It isn't what happens to you in life; it's how you deal with it." I made a decision to abandon my family and hang on to my old habits, so I blew the best thing that had happened to me. Today, I have to grin and bear it. Sherry is a pretty girl. She is so different from me. She's quiet and very attentive to Taron and Sky. Sky adores her. Every time jealousy creeps in, I remember how my daughter is being cared for and it brings a smile upon my face. If she didn't have a father like Taron, she would probably be in the system.

One day while visiting with Sky, John Jr. called me to see how things were progressing. "Hello Kyla, have you met my father yet?"

"John, I can't talk now, I'll have to call you at another time." While trying to whisper, Taron peeks at me from the corner of his eye. I did look rather sneaky, but I didn't want John to hear Sky in the background. I must have stirred up old feelings in Taron, because he walked Sky away from me and gave me a strange look. "Hey Taron, I'm not up to anything slick this time. I want to do the right thing. Can I please spend a little more time with her?"

"Kyla, I know you better than you think I do. Remember when I met you that night; you had that same look of desperation on your face. It scares me. I don't want Sky to get hurt."

"I promise Taron, I am going to stay out of trouble and get my life together. I want to do the right thing." Taron kissed me on the cheek and guided Sky towards me. "I trust you Kyla, don't let us down." The four of us had a great time together. Sherry and Taron explained to Sky that I was her biological mother and Sherry is the mother that will help take care of her. Her sweet little voice shouted, "So I will call you mommy and I'll call Sherry mommay." We all laughed and Sky gave me the biggest hug. At that moment, I felt life again. Her little hug reminded me of Frankie's hug when he was a little boy. Frankie would spoil Sky rotten if he was alive. As I was leaving, Sherry handed me a book. It looks like a spiritual book. I accepted it with a smile, but I said to myself, "If you want to give me something, just give me back my family." Then I was hit with a word from Frankie, "If you don't appreciate and treasure what God gives you, somebody else will." I came right back to reality and was thankful for Taron and Sherry.

I received my first paycheck and my first thought was that I could have made this money in a couple of hours. I could have hustled this out of someone. I then smiled and realized that I earned this honestly and this felt better than any scam that I pulled. I was able to buy my daughter gifts with legitimate money. Unlike, when I took care of Frankie, everything that I gave him was stolen. I guess that's why we never got the chance to really enjoy the material possessions. I would read my new book each day at lunch time. It was so peaceful. It is a book based completely on God and his purpose. I was really enjoying this book. I wish Frankie was here to enjoy this moment with me. I know he's getting a kick out of me. As time progressed, my diligence in my work paid off. I was promoted to perform duties within the main unit of the community. As I pushed my cart down the hall of "B" wing, I rolled by Judge's apartment.

"Hello Kayla." I looked to see where the deep proper voice was calling from. "That's not my name, my name is Kyla. There is no long 'a' sound. There is a long 'i' sound. It's Kyla."

"Hello Kyla. Are you assigned to clean my apartment today?"

"No, Unfortunately, I have not been promoted to enter the individual units. I'm assigned to clean the hallways."

"Why is that?"

"Why do you ask so many questions? But, if you must know I'm a bad girl and I guess they don't trust me. Oh... By the way, the rules state that I'm not supposed to talk to the residents."

"Now whose silly rule is that?"

"I don't know but it's in the handbook." I started to walk away, but Judge just kept on talking. I turned around and said, "Read my lips, I can't talk to you." I heard a voice interrupt me. It was an older lady that lived across the hall from Judge. "You heard her Judge. The help is not to socialize with the residents."

"I think I can handle this Betty, you can go into your apartment." I guess her co-signer didn't hear him because she continued on about the handbook and how the residents aren't supposed to mingle with the staff. The other old bag was checking me out from head to toe. She was looking at me as if I was trash. I gave her this look as if to say, "Yes, your white rich neighbor is interested in a poor black girl." I heard nosey Betty saying, "I'm surprised they would hire someone that looks like that." I wanted to smack her old ass. Judge must of have sensed that I was ready to tell her something then he continued with his conversation, "I won't tell, if you won't tell."

"You might not tell, but your nosey neighbors will." We both laughed. "They're the eyewitness news team." We laughed again. I enjoyed cleaning the courtyard because I got to listen to everyone stories.

Miles had to have the best job in this place. Apparently,

he is the Judge's wife private care giver, but he always seemed to be playing games and enjoying himself. He must tell Judge everything. I overheard him telling Judge how his adopted father confronted him about looking for his biological parents. "Hey Judge, would you be insulted if your adopted son was interested in locating his parents?"

"It all depends; I don't have any adopted children, so I can't answer that."

"Last night while I was listening to Kirk Walum, I decided to Google search my parents. While I was on the computer, my father knocked on the door. He wanted to know what was on my mind and I told him. He said the information that he has on my parents were their last known place of residence; Chester, Pennsylvania and the adoption agency was not allowed to give out any more information. I asked him how he would feel about me looking for my parents and he made me feel guilty as hell."

He said, "Miles, I love you and we've always tried to give you the best. I want you to do whatever makes you happy." Then he left the room.

"Your father loves you and he doesn't want you to get hurt, why can't you just leave well enough alone?"

"I need to do this. It is possible that in order to get the answers I am seeking, I will need to cut back my hours at the nursing home."

"Oh my…I was hoping that you would be able to pick up a few extra days with Mrs. Chapman. She needs more care. The administrator has another complaint about her and you seem to be the only person that can keep her calm."

"What is it now?"

"Last evening while everyone was eating dinner, Mrs. Chapman went to each room and stripped the beds. Then she hid all the linens and wouldn't tell anyone where she had put them. When I asked her about the situation, she just sat in her chair and smiled."

"Wow, her dementia is getting that bad huh?"

"I don't believe she has dementia, I believe she gets a kick out of humiliating and embarrassing me."

"Now why would she want to do that?"

"It's too personal and complex to explain. It has to do with my past. Well anyway, do you think you can help me out? The administrator is threatening to move her out of the facility."

"You can't let him do that."

"I told him if he moves her out of here, then he'll never work as an administrator in this business again."

"What was his response?"

"He didn't say anything, but I was told that he said he's tired of working for us rich bastards."

"Strong words coming from someone that earns his living. I'll let you know how many days I can give you."

"She's really starting to wear me out."

"You don't really believe that she knows what she's doing do you? She's been diagnosed with dementia"

"I believe she's very aware of what she's doing. She holds a lot of resentment in her heart for me. I've always loved her, but I was never the husband that I've should have been to her."

"No need to explain. I understand." I walked by bopping my head to my IPOD. I saw the both of them watching me like a hawk. I started dancing and dusting at the same time. I heard Judge say, "She seem like a nice girl. You should ask her out."

"She's fine as hell, but she's too ghetto for me. My parent's wouldn't trust the sight of her."

"Do you require your parent's approval for a date?"

"No, but I respect their opinions. I once dated a girl whose style was similar to hers, and my parents would actually make her clap if she was left alone in one of our rooms." A loud burst of laughter covered the air.

"Why would they make her clap?"

"They felt the clapping would hinder her from stealing anything."

"Please tell me that you're joking."

"Yes, I am joking, but they watched her like a hawk." I gave him a nasty look to let him know that I heard what he had said. His face turned red. I rolled my eyes and walked away. I thought to myself just who in the hell does he think he is? I can't stand people that pass judgment on people they don't even know. Maybe, just maybe, this is why his parents gave him up for adoption. They knew he was going to be a jackass. I wish Frankie was around to check this joker. I don't have time to feed into small nonsense. But this crap would be right up Frankie's alley. As I was vacuuming, I could feel someone starring at me from the other end of the hall. I finally made my way by Judge's apartment. "Hello Mr. Judge."

"Everybody calls me Judge. Would you like something to drink?"

"I can't drink on the job."

He laughs then says, "I was thinking more like a soft drink."

"Do you have any Kool-Aid?" He gives me a blank stare. I nudged him on the shoulder, "I'm just joking, and you wouldn't know anything about Kool-Aid. What else do you have?"

"Come in I'm sure I can find something for you." I was very hesitant. I looked around each corner then I hid my cart in the utility closet. When Judge noticed that I was hesitant, he said, "It's only for a minute, I'm not going to bite you."

"I'm not afraid of you biting me; I have teeth, so therefore I will bite you back." I was amazed with each step that I took. "Wow this place is off the hook, and this TV is the bomb." Judge looked at me as if I was talking Greek. With laughter, he said, "What did you say?"

I covered my mouth to hide my embarrassment. "I'm sorry; you have a really nice place."

"Thank you. Where are you from?"

"I'm from Pennsylvania."

"What brings you to Delaware?"

"I go where the wind blows." He smiled as he handed me my glass of juice. I could not stop admiring his apartment. It looked as if it was a model apartment. Nothing was out of order. I couldn't help but to ask about the beautiful painting of an equally beautiful young woman. Before I could get my words out, Judge explained, "This is my wife." He pointed to the huge painting as if it was on exhibit. "She was in her early twenties when she posed for this painting. Those were the good old days."

"And what does that suppose to mean?"

He walked up to me and avoided my question. In a soothing voice he said, "I think you're a pretty young lady."

"I think that you're wife is pretty too. You are still married, aren't you?

"Yes, I am. I've been married for over forty years. My wife is very ill. She lives here on the health care unit. She has a condition that causes her not to remember much."

Very sarcastically I said, "She has dementia or Alzheimer."

In his surprisingly voice, "Yes, that's it."

"I'm sorry to hear that. So does that make it okay for you to flirt with other woman?" He looked at me, smiled and said, "No it doesn't."

I took another sip of my juice and blurted out, "Can I ask you a question?"

"Shoot"

"How can you wake up to the same old face for all of those years? I think that would bore the hell out of me."

"Yes, it can be boring, but sometimes people can't always have what excites them all of the time. It's called life." I smiled, put my glass down and thanked him for the juice. "If you get thirsty tomorrow, remember it's free refills."

"Thanks."

I found myself walking away with a very sexy strut. I felt as though, just maybe, I was becoming attractive to this man. I had to do a reality check. This was business; business only. But deep down, I've always had a passion for older men. Some may label it as a father-daughter syndrome; especially since I lost my own father at a very young age. I have always long for that protection of a father. Ironically, Frankie believed that I was searching for that father figure; father replacement. Maybe? Maybe not? In any event, I realized that older men seem to cater to younger women more. They're more understanding. They know their place with younger women and do not mind relinquishing control. I certainly love having control. That characteristic is power to me and I enjoy power.

6

Miles pulls out the piece of paper that his father gave him. He walks into an old brick building. The receptionist looks at him over top of her glasses. With a country accent, "May I help you?"

"Yes, my name is Miles Porter and I was adopted in 1986. I would like to find my biological parents."

The old lady extends her hand. She reads the paper that Miles gave her. She looks at him and says, "Kevin Johnson, born December 7, 1984."

"Yes maam, that's correct."

"Please have a seat and I'll be right back. Can I see your identification please?"

Miles waits patiently until the lady returns with his paperwork. He reads the paper with a look of suspense on his face. His echo fills the room. "Kevin and Kyle Johnson, born December 7, 1984. Born at Crozer Hospital, Chester, Pennsylvania. Parents are Kevin and Tracey Johnson." I have a brother, a twin brother. I wonder where he's at. Miles heads straight to Crozer Hospital.

He's curious and anxious about finding his parents. A very cute and sexy receptionist consciously performs her duties at the desk. Miles approaches the desk and introduces himself. He hands her the birth certificate. The sexy receptionist leans towards him and smile. "I'm sorry, but we no longer have this information on record. It is now on microfilm, and that will take at least three weeks for us to locate." Miles closes his eyes and walks away. As he's leaving the building, the receptionist runs through the doors waving for him to come back. Miles freezes in his footsteps. Secretively, she leans forward; her breast brushing lightly against his chest and whispers, "Chester is very small and everyone knows each other. There's a very large family with the last name of Johnson. They live off of ninth and Yearn streets. The area is rough and the family can be rougher."

"And what does that suppose to mean?"

"Just be careful. If you get scared or lost, you know where to find me."

"Thanks, can I have your number?"

"Is it for a date or for your protection?"

"Both." She smiles and hands Miles a piece of paper. Miles gives her a friendly wink and walks triumphantly towards his vehicle. As he drives through Chester, he notices the graffiti on the walls, the trash, and the old abandon houses. A group of guys are playing basketball and another group of guys are hanging on the corner. Miles gets out of his jeep. He notices a drug transaction taking place. "What the hell is this?" He gets back in his jeep and drives away. He notices a group of old men sitting on an old torn down bench. They look to be in their late seventies. He gets out and walks towards them.

"Good afternoon gentlemen. Can you please tell me where I can find the Johnson family?"

A man with a southern accent speaks up, "Oh that girl has burnt you for some money too huh? "She's too fast; you'll never catch her. You'll have to wait in line. She's real slick."

All of the men start to laugh. Miles speaks up, "Catch who? What are you talking about?"

Another man interrupts, "Whatever her name is. The pretty gal. The one with a large collection of males pursuing her for one reason or another. She uses them for money then she vanishes." The man is spitting and talking at the same time. He is so excited. His friends are in agreement with him. Miles breaks up the show.

"No, I'm not looking for whoever this girl is. I'm looking for Kevin and Tracey Johnson."

The man with the southern accent interrupts, "Oh boy, you're going way back. That boy is in jail. He killed some girl over dope." His friends shake their heads in agreement. "Y'all know what I'm talking about. That killing that happened in Philadelphia a long time ago."

Another man joins in, "Oh, I remember…you are talking about Geraldine's youngest boy. That whole family was trouble." Miles walks away from the conversation.

7

As I prance across the courtyard, I can't help to notice the three musketeers sitting in the courtyard. Miles, Judge and his wife are enjoying a day in the sun. Miles seems to be a bit occupied. Mrs. Chapman picks a flower from the garden and hands it to him. "Thank you, Mrs. Chapman. This is one of the nicest things someone has ever done for me." Miles places a kiss on her cheek. Mrs. Chapman smiles and walks away. Judge interferes with the scene. "Are you okay Miles? She must sense that something is wrong with you."

"I have a lot on my mind, but I told you before that there's nothing wrong with Mrs. Chapman. She has plenty of sense."

Judge burst into laughter. "You think so."

"I know so."

"Well enough of talking about her. How are you doing?"

"Not so good. I found out that I have a brother. Correction, a twin brother that I never knew existed. I have a dead mother, and a convict for a father." Miles conversation went to complete silence. I can feel Judge starring at me. It was something about him that made him attractive. He possessed a strong sense of security and confidence. That was always a turn on for me. Frankie possessed some of the same unique qualities. He was always comfortable with himself. It didn't matter that he was parentless most of his life, abused as a child, or an addict. Whatever state of mind he was in, he still knew that it was something greater at the end of the rainbow. I miss him so much. While Judge was starring, so was Mrs. Chapman. She watched her husband as he watched me. I was becoming very uncomfortable. I heard her say, "Miles finish your conversation, I'm listening to you."

I left the courtyard and went to the main building to finish my work. Judge must of have run over to the building before me. As I was walking up the hallway, he opened his door. He had the nerve to signal for me to come in. I turned around and looked back as if he was talking to someone else. He smiled, "I'm talking to you miss." I did not want the nosey neighbor to come out so I decided to go in to see what he wanted. "Are you thirsty?"

"Yes, I can use a drink." He hands me a tall glass of lemonade and an envelope at the same time. I was surprised. I opened the envelope and inside was a gift card to FYE music store.

"Why did you give me this?"

"I noticed that you're always listening to music, so I thought that you might be able to use this."

I handed it back to him. "I can't take this, I might get fired."

"Who's going to tell?"

"Do you hand out gifts cards to everyone?"

"No, not really. But, if they can make my heart smile, I probably would."

"That's really cute. I like that. Since that's the case, I'll take it." He shakes his head and smiles at me. "Okay this has been fun, but I must get back to work."

"Can you stop by when you get off?"

"I'll have to think about it." A loud outburst sounded

from my walkie talkie. “Kyla, please go to the third floor of the health care unit. I need you up there.” When I arrived on the third floor, I thought I was in the land of the lost. Old people were wandering around in circles. Some were eating, some were talking to themselves, and some were just sitting and starring. It was scary. I didn’t know that dementia was this deep. As I was cleaning up the spill, a lady walked over to me and dumped spaghetti all over me. When I cleared my view, I noticed that it was Mrs. Chapman. She was laughing as she was walking away. My first instinct was to whip her old ass, but I instantly thought of Sky. I would go back to jail with no get out of jail free card. The staff tried to convince me that she was unaware of her behavior, but I couldn’t buy that. “If she’s unaware of her behavior and her thoughts, how can she remember to tell me that her husband is a nigga lover?”

The two white nurses were very embarrassed. I walked over to Judge’s apartment to ask if he’d mine if I cleaned myself up. Judge was trying to hold in his laugh when he saw me. “What happen to you?” This crazy ass lady poured her food on me. She better be glad that she’s old or I would of have whipped her ass.”

Judge is standing still with a blank stare on his face. “Was it the woman who sits outside with me?”

“I believe so.”

Judge sighs, “Please forgive her, that’s my wife and she has dementia. She’s really not aware of what she does.”

I looked at him as if to say yeah right. “Let me make it up to you.”

“Nah, I’m cool. I just need to take a shower. Luckily I have a change of clothes in my bag. Do you mind if I clean myself up.”

"Go right ahead." Judge showed me to the shower and handed me a towel and washcloth. It felt good to take a long hot shower in his marble finished bathroom. The shower head was huge; the water covered my entire body. I loved the way his fluffy Ralph Lauren towel felt against my body. I dried off, changed into my fitted jeans and tank top. I blow dried my hair bone straight and freshened up my face. When I walked in the room, Judge smiled at me.

"You look lovely. Would you like to order something to eat?"

"I would love a cold glass of wine first." He picked up the remote control, aimed it towards the television and ordered a bottle of wine.

"It must be nice to have everything right at your finger tips."

Judge smirked and said, "Oh trust me, I don't have everything at my finger tips and being wealthy has its ups and downs. Now what would you like to eat, Miss?"

"You choose." Before I could finish my walk through the beautiful apartment, the doorbell was ringing. Not only did they deliver quickly, the waiter also set up the delicious meal for us. I watched from the balcony as the waiter performed as if he was in a luxury restaurant. The food was very attractive looking. It looked almost too good to eat.

"What is this?"

"It's a fish taco salad." I was hesitant at first but I was also hungry. We both sat down to eat. Judge went directly to his food. I grab his hand so he couldn't eat his food.

"Do you mind if I bless the food first?"

"Not at all."

After I blessed the food, we laughed and talked for

hours. He explained his relationship concerning Miles. He told me that Miles was the son that he wished that he had. He told me about his tenuous relationship with his two sons. He also told me that he has always had an infatuation with women of color and that he hasn't had a sexual relationship with his wife in years. I found our conversation to be very interesting. I didn't share much of my life with him. I figured he wouldn't understand it, so why bother. I also felt that when people hear about my story, they tend to feel guilty about all of the unnecessary complaining that they put out. Judge didn't say much about his children. I found this to be rather strange. He has two sons. All men are usually proud of their sons. As openly as he expressed his personal feelings and relationships, I still felt that he was suffering from something but, I didn't know what.

As I was leaving his apartment, he kissed me on my cheek. I couldn't help but notice the music that he was listening to. "What are you listening to?"

"I'm listening to Classic R&B." A big chuckle came from my mouth.

"What do you know about R&B?"

"Everything, I listen to all sorts of music, classical, reggae, you name it."

I continued to laugh. I was smiling and blushing at the same time. This old man was very smooth. He had a Sean Connery, James Bond persona. He was very sexy for an older man. I broke up my thoughts by blurting out, "Please don't put on any classical music that makes me sleepy." We both laughed. I should have left the apartment. But, I did not; something kept me there. I did not require a script to know how it was going to play out. Although our conversation was friendly, I was starting to question myself. What was I getting into? I was a lot of things in my life, but never a mistress and besides, I slept with his married son. I was starting to question the deal that I agreed to with John Jr. After lying there for two minutes, I jumped up, ran to the bedroom, grabbed my clothes and ran to the door.

"Where are you going?"

"I have to leave now; my train stops running in an hour. I also have to check on my daughter."

Before Judge could get another word out, I was out the door. As I walked down the hall, I kept hearing little voices, saying that, "You said you were not going to live like this anymore. You are worth more than this; you are a decent, respectable young lady now. Your tricking days are behind you."

I heard Frankie's voice over and over, "You get what you get because you do what you do." I was driving myself crazy. I let out an annoying frustrating scream as I walked out of the building. I looked around very quickly to see if any one was watching me. I felt like a real nut. Immediately, I telephoned John Jr. to see if it was anything else that I could do to get custody of my daughter.

"Hi John, how are you?"

"I'm great are you handling your business?"

I took a deep long breath. "John, I was wondering if there is anything else that I can do to settle our agreement."

"When I tried to love you, you wouldn't let me. Therefore, I don't know any other options but to stick to the plan. Remember, those were your words."

"John, I don't think I can go along with this. Your father seems to be too nice of a guy."

"I understand. Umm…Apparently, he has your ass fooled too. He's a selfish, inconsiderate bastard and he's going to pay for the way he treated us. Besides, when have you become so sensitive to other people's feelings?"

"Forget it John, We'll stick to the plan." I hung the phone up in his ear. He was right, when did I become so damn sensitive? I guess that spiritual book was working on me. I was starting to soften up. If I want custody of my daughter, I must rid myself of this 'goodie-two shoes" attitude and be what I know I can be…a player.

8

My probation officer was really cool. Ms. Neils was so down to earth. She made it clear that she was more than a probation officer. She was working here because she wanted hands on for helping people get their lives together and more importantly, stay together. I was to report to her once a week. She's very attractive and she's about her business. I would love to know her annual salary. This woman dresses as if she's modeling for Ebony Fashion Fair or something. I have yet to see a piece of hair out of place. I know good clothes, because I sold clothes on the streets for years. I can look at a suit and name the designer. She is just pure class. I'm surprised to see her not wearing a wedding band. She's probably too much for one man. She doesn't say much, but she speaks with a lot of knowledge about the streets.

"Hello Kyla, I'm assigned as your probation officer. I would also like to be your mentor. I studied your case and your life; I would like to assist in getting your life on track. Do you have any questions?"

"Just one. How much does this job pay? I know a lot about fashion. Your suit probably cost more than your weekly paycheck." She gave me a smirk of a smile.

"Anymore questions?"

"Nope. Maybe you should inform me of the rules of

my probation."

"Well…First, I think it is only fair that you know a little something about me. It will make our relationship much easier. Beside the fancy suit, there is a little more to me. I will give you some background on myself. If you must know I'm also a psychiatrist. So not only will you report to me to stay out of jail, but you can also discuss any issues that you would like. If you don't feel comfortable talking to me, we can work around it. You are not the only parolee that I have mentored and counseled. There are several others, but three very special ladies are my personal success stories."

"Three success stories. Wow! I'm sure you can hardly wait to tell me about them."

"I'm very proud of them and their lives. Today, they are all married and have dedicated their lives to the Lord."

"Umm…before you start, I am not that sort of individual…how would you say it…umm…born again, holy roller; so I would appreciate if you don't push your values on me."

"No problem. Let's start from the beginning. Although I have read your file, it is possible that the whole story is not being told here. Do you wish to give me your story? Start anywhere."

"Well…Should I start with the death of my mother? The incarceration of my father? The separation of my brother? I have a checkerboard life. Maybe the many foster homes and the abuse can give you the real story of me!

"I understand your anger. That's perfectly normal. You must believe me when I tell you that I am not here to pass judgment. I am here with all sincerity to help you."

"I'm…sorry for being so abrupt. I'm mad…Maybe

just at the wrong people."

"Who should you be mad at?"

There was silence for a moment. Kyla stared out of the window wishing she was somewhere else; anywhere but there. "Excuse me Kyla; you seem to have drifted off. Who should you be mad at? It should not be difficult to answer. It is evident that the system failed both you and your brother. Are you mad at the system?"

"Maybe."

"In my book that is progress. The system should have devised a way to keep you and your brother together. Sometimes it is difficult when the children are older. Unfortunately, homes prefer to take in infants or toddlers. Your ages made it difficult."

As Ms. Neil continued to look into Kyla's face, she witnessed a change in the surface. "Life has been unnecessarily cruel and unfair. Some people go through life without a care in the world; I on the other hand, encountered my fair share and then some. Maybe…Some of my misfortune was a direct result of my inability to let go. Damn…look, just give me the rules and let me go about my business."

Ms. Neil realized that Kyla was going to be a tough one to penetrate. There were far too many scars, but she was certain that she would be able to turn her life around.

"You know Kyla if you give the system a chance and by system, I mean me, a chance, I just may be able to get you on the right track. I do have several success stories."

"I'm sure you have many stories. But, I'm not interested."

My sessions with my probation officer became very therapeutic. I know she has a daughter because of the beautiful pictures of a little girl in her office. She paints vivid pictures about life, by using other people's lives. She seems to be very protective about her story. My intuition tells me that she has a hell of a story. She reminds me a lot of Frankie, always trying to get into my head, but keeping her secrets to herself. I believe that's why I like her; she keeps me thinking about Frankie. I call her P.O. for short. That stands for probation officer. She gets a big kick out of me. She tells me that I remind her of three protégés that she mentors. These three girls were off the hook. I thought I was a beast in the streets. She begins by telling me the background of three of her successes.

"You see…I formed a special bond with the three ladies…Kinda, Lala, and Ness. All three of them are integral parts of my life. They had it hard. They grew up in the projects of Philadelphia and they matured in those same projects. During my relationship with them, I attempted to polish down their negative aspects; especially their project lives. On the other hand, I wanted to promote their best qualities. The most important quality all three of them had were their minds not their bodies. We had many special moments. I introduced them to the finer things in life. We exchanged laughter for the good times and tears for the few sad times. These three ladies were very special ladies. They were fighters. Unfortunately, their energies were used the wrong way. They were involved in street brawls…Some over men and some with men."

"It's amazing that there is always a man involved when a woman is messed up."

"That's not the case at all. These women, all three, possessed very strong personalities. These three put the gold in gold digging. They were atypical. Early on in their lives, they made plans to escape poverty. Would you like to know the most important aspect of their lives?"

"I'm sure you are going to tell me."

"Umm…their friendship. The bond between them was unbreakable. No man, money, or circumstance could break that bond. Although you are one, you have a bond and it is with your brother. I know that you don't want me to push my beliefs upon you, but trust me and trust God. When the time is right, God will reunite you with your brother. Your bond will be solidified."

"Yeah…yeah. Any more stories or can I leave now?" That's probably why I'm a loner and handles all my business by myself. I never had a friend that I can trust besides Frankie and I couldn't take him on any jobs because he spent more time analyzing the job than he did watching my back. I asked her what happened to these girls and where are they now.

"Be patient. I have a few more stories to share. Today, all three ladies have committed their lives to Christ. That's why I know that God is real. In my profession, I meet all sorts of people with all sorts of stories. The most promiscuous girl that I knew became celibate for an entire year after finding a relationship with God. In the past, she treated all men like a bank and if they wanted to play they knew that they would have to pay. She went from a gold digging, material girl to marrying a pastor. She now submits to him, I don't say that in a bad way, but it's a good thing to see her think of someone other than herself. It shows growth and maturity on her part. She now realizes that she no longer has to control a man with her looks and her body. She was very intimidating to men. She could have made a prince feel like a frog in a blink of an eye. All of them felt a need to possess her; unfortunately, I didn't see one of them succeed. She always had the mind for business. Today, she runs the business of her husband's mega church. She also teaches the young women ministry with her other two friends. The turnout is phenomenal. They all have powerful testimonies and they don't hold back anything. They are really touching the lives of these young sistas and that's what church should be about, to help change lives.

Lala, one of my special young ladies, was always the voice of reasoning but she did have her weaknesses. Unfortunately, it was her man. He was the love of her life. She granted him free range in the relationship. She was a better woman than most. I admired her zeal to hang tight in her relationship. Her man cheated but she stayed. Kinda, Ness, and I did not understand why she accepted his behavior nor did we ask. She was the better player at her own game. She knew, in time, he would be hers. At the end, the queen captured her king. By the way, her husband is a living testimony to this day."

"Really!"

"He was a player in more ways than one. He got caught up in the street game and that game just about did him in. His bullet ridden body was delivered to the hospital where doctors informed him that he would never walk again or be able to conceive children. But *The Glory be to God*, he is not only walking, he is running. Today, they are proud parents of a beautiful set of twins and Lala is pregnant as we speak. Jay, her husband, took all his street knowledge and turned it into a multi-million dollar business. He was given a second chance at life and he gives others a second chance. He employs ex-drug dealers, ex-cons, and all others with prison records. This is his ministry. You see, all we need is a second chance."

"Wow! That's deep."

"I noticed that I have your attention. There's more. Ness was the most difficult case. It took her awhile to surrender her will to God. Honestly, it took her near death to realize that love is not supposed to hurt. After getting beat near death by her drug-crazed boyfriend, she finally turned her life over. She's on fire for God. She teaches a self esteem class to teens. Her husband loves the ground that she walks on. She found out that she was pregnant two days after her wedding. They both were ecstatic until the child came out looking like her ex-lover. I admire her honesty. She had informed me that it was a strong possibility that Craig was not the father of her child. She didn't cheat on him, but Gary raped her prior to the stabbing. Craig is a very supportive husband and at that time, he told her that abortion was not an option. Their relationship is amazing. It must be true what they say about feeding a child; if you feed a child long enough, that he'll start to look like you. I swear, little Craig is starting to look just like Big Craig."

I listened tentatively as she continued to speak. I was mesmerized by her story. Briefly, she spoke on how they helped her get back on track. I could not believe that she was ever off track. There lies the mystery. A part of me wanted to know the intricate details, but I would save it for another time. Time was what the two of us had in common. She spoke candidly of life, relationships, and God. I was almost sorry that our session was coming to an end."

"Well, Kyla, our time is up today. Much was said here today and I hope you take some knowledge with you. Remember, the bible says people perish from the lack of knowledge. So, being ignorant or ignoring and pretending not to know something can hurt you. It also states, 'In all doings, get understanding.' You have your instructions and please, if you need me for anything; any time of day or night, just call. I'm here for you. I'll see you next week and please have a good one"

"You do the same." In the back of my mind, I felt there was a deeper story to her. She had an aura about her. I still have keen street smarts and game recognizes game. I understand that her agenda is to do her job but… there is sincerity in her words. I think I will feel comfortable talking to her. She appears to be quite interesting.

Since our initial meeting, I have grown rather fond of Ms. Neils. She has a way of pulling out the best and the worst of people. She is so unique. She studies me during the sessions and I know it is for my best interest. After each session, we will hug as we said our goodbyes for the day. I always come away learning more and more about me. I grew to understand and believe that I had a chance at life if I just gave me a chance. If Lala, Kinda, and Ness can change their lives, then I know that I can change mine.

9

Weeks had gone by since Miles had tried to find his biological parents. He sits in his room with a telephone directory and a list of prisons. He dials the telephone numerous times before he gets a live person on the other end. “Hello I’m looking for an inmate by the name of Kevin Johnson.”

“Hold on please.” He sits with his fingers crossed as he listens to his Jazz.

“Yes, we have a couple of inmates by that name. Do you have a date of birth or an inmate number?”

“Miss, I don’t have either one, my situation is rather complex. I know my father’s name but have no other vital information. Can you help me?”

“Well without either pertinent information, your best bet is to visit the prison and complete some paperwork. That can be a start. From that point, we may be able to assist you.”

Miles hangs up the telephone. He is very anxious and uncertain that he is doing the right thing. He paces the floor as he practices what to say to his long lost father. Early the next morning, he rises and prepare for his drive to the prison. . During his journey, he’s constantly rehearses his lines while worrying about his biological father’s reception. When he reaches the old crusty building that reads “Graterford.”

Chills radiates through his entire body. He approaches the information desk and informs them of his situation. He completes the necessary papers and is shown to a room. Nervously, he takes stock of his surroundings. Many other people are sitting where he waits. Unlike him, they appear more comfortable. Miles waits patiently while this tall once handsome man is escorted to the table for which he sits. Suspiciously, the gentleman examines Miles,

"Hello sir, my name is Miles." Miles extends his hand to the gentleman.

"Hello, I'm Kevin." He shakes Miles hand.

"This is going to sound really crazy but I believe that I'm your son."

"I don't have a son named Miles."

"Miles is my adopted name. My birth name is Kevin."

Kevin reaches for Miles left arm and smirks. "What are you looking for?"

"You were burnt by an iron when you were two years old. I'm looking for the scar."

"What makes you think the scar would still be here."

"That was a very nasty burn, I'm sure it would of have left a mark."

"I always wondered what this scar was."

Kevin stands up and gives Miles a hug. He became very emotional. At last, he has a chance to fuse his past with his present. It's been a long time and his pain had encrusted his memories of that awful night.

"Who adopted you?"

"I have two great parents. I must say that I have been extremely fortunate. Earlier this year, they decided to inform me that I was adopted. Without hesitation and much contemplation, I decided to search for my parents."

"Well…Um…I'm sorry to disappoint you. Certainly,

this is not what you have expected. Do you know my story?"

"Not exactly."

"What happened to my mother, and how much time do you have in here."

"Well…I stop counting the time. I was given a twenty year sentence and your mother was murdered."

"Did you murder her?" Kevin takes a deep breath.

"To be perfectly honest with you, I can't remember anything about that night. The only thing I remember is that your mother was the prettiest lady I've ever laid my eyes on. I adored her, but we were both addicted to crack and we were living very sinful lives. I want you to believe me when I tell you that I can't remember killing her."

"I'm not sure I fully understand. Did you ever hit her?"

"I've never laid a hand on her, but I do take responsibility for killing her soul. I introduced her to crack. As far as I'm concern, that is as good as murder."

"Did you love her?"

"I still love her. I think about her everyday and I pray to God that she forgives me for leading her into that terrible life."

"I understand that I have a twin brother."

"No you have a twin sister."

"The birth certificate says the name Kyle."

"Her name is Kyla. They must of have made a mistake. Doing that time, our life was in so much turmoil neither your mother nor I did what was right by you two."

"Do you have any idea where I can find her?" Before Kevin can answer, a big officer walks over to their table. "Time's up buddy." Kevin and Miles embrace each other and smile.

"Is it okay if I come back to visit you?"

"Sure, I'd love that." Kevin approaches the officer. "Can I leave money on Kevin books?"

"You'll have to put it in a money order. Are you related to him?"

"Yes I am."

"Kevin is a good brother. I always wondered why he doesn't get any visits. It's good to see you, make sure you come back to see him."

"I will, thanks man."

One thing I learned while being in the joint was to stay true to my word. Michelle asked me to do her a favor and that was to secure a job for her brother. Unfortunately her brother had served time for check fraud and was paroled a month prior to my release. Me, myself, and I should be my main concern but a promise is a promise. I didn't know how I was going to get him a job, but I was going to try my best. The only job I've ever had was working for the telemarketing company and those type companies do perform criminal background checks. As an adult, your criminal record is not suppressed like that of a juvenile. As much as I hated to, John Jr. was my one and only resource. He's a big player in Philly and he's well connected to the unions. I'll just have to swallow my pride and go into debt for another favor.

"Hi John this is "Kyla".

"My, my, my…What do I owe the honor of this call?"

"I need a favor from you."

"You need a favor from me, imagine that. Meet me at the Lowes Hotel and we can talk about it."

"The hell with you John." I hung the phone up and hated myself for even calling him. I want to help Michelle, but I'm already in debt with this devil. My cell phone was blowing up. I refuse to answer it. When I finally got up the nerve to answer the phone, there read a text message from John. 6:00 pm at the Lowes Hotel on Market Street. That was my biggest attraction about John Jr. He is so damn cocky and confident. It has been a year since we indulged in each other and that was the last time I was intimate with anyone. I was mad and confused as I drove to Philadelphia. I am already indebted to him. My priority is my child. Loyalty is one thing but this…Uh…it is making me sick just thinking about my payment for a favor. Was I that loyal to Michelle or did I still hold a crush for this asshole.

As I walked in the hotel lobby, there sat one of the most handsome men I've ever laid eyes on. I must admit, damn he is good looking. I must keep my head straight. I must keep it business no pleasure…Umm…umm…The hotel was more busy than usual. Some sort of convention was being held and it was full hustle and bustle. I watched each lady that walked by John Jr. admire his swagger. He still was picture perfect and had teeth that lit up the room. I inhaled his Jean Paul Gaultier fragrance from across the room. He knows that aroma turns me on.

"Hey beautiful!"

"Hi John."

"Take a seat, we have all night. What can I get you to drink?"

"I'll take an Apple Martini"

"Make it a double, please."

"John I'm not here to play games with you, I need a favor."

"What can I do for you sweetie?"

"Let's not get so personal, okay." John let out a burst of laughter. "I need you to find a job for a friend of mine. He's a good dude and he's raising my friend's children."

"What kind of skills does he carry?"

"I'm not quite sure but I do recall her saying that he's good with his hands."

"Good hands, umm…Have him give me a call tomorrow. As a matter of fact, have him go to Local 332 union hall. If he goes to the business office and ask for Bryant, he'll take good care of him."

"Just like that?"

"Yes, just like that! "Local 332 has been known for helping and restoring the lives of many. They've supported me when I was running for Judge. Well enough about me. You look great. Apparently, a little jail time only enhances your appearance. You are rather stunning if you permit me to render you a compliment. You know I miss you."

Those Apple Martinis must have been very strong because I caught myself thinking that I was beginning to miss him too. I hurried up and swallowed my second drink. "We still have time to catch a meal. I have back stage passes for the stage play *The Color Purple.* "Well, I am hungry and I've wanted to see that play for the longest, so what the hell." John and I had a great time that night. Why couldn't the favor, the dinner and the play be enough for me? I always have to play with fire. When I woke up in the next morning, I was pleased, but at the same time, angry that I fell for this man again. I left the hotel before he had awakened. I know that John is a man of his word, so he'll call the union and make things happen.

Just when I was trying to do right, wrong was there to steer me wrong. One of Frankie's favorite people from the bible was Paul. I did like hearing about Paul. In Romans 7:19, Paul said, *For the Good that I would I do not; But the evil which I would not; that I do.* I am beginning to feel like Paul.

It's been two years now and I haven't had a physical

fight. I've come close but I was always able to pull back. I am already feeling like crap after sleeping with John Jr. and I bumped into the big Amazon chick from the prison. I am not a punk, but I figured that I would try to avoid her. I knew it was going to be hard. Unfortunately, she's not the forgiving type. I whipped her ass once and it was ugly. To stay out of trouble, I have to keep my head on straight. I crossed the street when I noticed her and her girlfriends walking on Market Street. I can tell they were just coming off of a beat, so I figured that she wouldn't want to draw any attention to herself. I put on my shades and pretended to window shop.

"Yo…hold up, I think that's the chick I was telling you about from the prison. Her name is "Kyla".

I heard a squeaky voice giggle, "I know that tiny ass girl did not leave you scarred like that."

"I told you that she hit me with a metal phone. Well we are not in the joint now, so now I'll see what she's about."

"Come on girl this ain't worth it. We have over ten thousand dollars of illegal goods on us, save your little petty beef for another time." I felt a sigh of relief when I heard her say that. I know I was changing or at least I was growing up. I did not feel like fighting. Then I heard a revengeful voice, "Hell no, I'm going to handle this now." I began to walk faster. The faster I walked the faster they came. "Hey "Kyla", what's up?

"Nothing."

"Remember me."

"Yeah I remember you. Hey, the past is the past. Let bygone be bygone. I want no trouble and I'm sure you don't want any. Let's just move on." Before I can get out another word, I felt a hard pound on the side of my head. I dropped my pocket book and we were tangling. She felt even bigger this time around. My adrenaline wasn't as high as before. I felt every punch that her and her girlfriends threw. I had no idea an ass whipping can feel like this. I was out of breath, air and energy. I felt like I was on a roller coaster ride. It was hard to believe no one was going to break this fight up. It wasn't a fight it was a massacre. The only thing I had left in me was prayer. I couldn't believe that she was not getting tired. She was the one doing all of the work. I think I threw about five punches; but four of them hit the air. That really took the wind out of me. For the first time in my life, I was happy to hear sirens.

"Okay ladies, break it up." I was thinking to myself, "She's the only one fighting." By then her girlfriends, must of put the stolen goods in my pocketbook. When the officer finally was able to peel her off of me, I thought I was in the next week. I was totally disoriented. The other officer felt sorry for me, so he picked up my pocketbook and put me in his patrol car. He gave me a towel to wipe the blood off of my face. When I looked in the mirror, I was terrified, I had a large cut over the top of my eye and I had enough scratches on my face to play Tic Tac Toe. I combed my hair and it was shedding like a cat. I glanced at that big Amazon and she appeared as if she had just gotten dressed. The officer continued to talk to the girls outside the car.

"May I see some identification ladies?" They all began to look in their pocketbooks. One of the girls gave me a very sarcastic look. I quickly picked up her vibe and I looked in my pocketbook. Inside was a lot of rings and jewelry. "I'll be damned." My entire life flashed in front of me. "Sky, Taron, my job!" What the hell was I was going to do. The only thing I did know was I was not going back to jail. One of the girls began to resist arrest.

Her antics gave me enough time to get rid of the stolen jewelry. I lifted up the mats on the floor of the car and put some of the jewelry under there. I stuffed the rest of it under the driver's seat. While I was kicking the jewelry under the seat the officer was walking towards the patrol car. "Young lady are you okay?"

"I'll be fine officer; I just need to get home to my daughter."

"Would you like to press charges against these young ladies?"

"Officer, I'm, fine. I need to go."

"Let me see your identification so I can make a police report in case you change your mind." I gave him the necessary information and I was headed on my way. I couldn't wait to get home. My entire body was aching. I was emotionally and physically drained. My opponents weren't as lucky as I was; when I looked back, the three of them were being taken away in handcuffs.

***

Judge is walking through the healthcare unit to visit with Mrs. Chapman. He's approached by the nursing home administrator. "Hello Judge, do you have a minute to chat?"

"Yes, how can I help you?"

"Are you aware of your wife's incident yesterday?"

"Yes, I am aware."

"Unfortunately, your wife is becoming more agitated with our staff and I'm afraid she's going to hurt someone; if not my staff then maybe another resident."

"So, what are you saying?"

"You might want to consider getting her more hours

with her private duty nurse."

"What are my options?"

"I would have to ask you to remove her from the facility if you don't get her more help."

"If you do that, I promise you that you will never work in any nursing home again."

"Miles…"

"I need for you to understand. We have many more patients with equal needs as your wife. It is not like our institution has not been more than patient with Mrs. Champman. In any event, Miles is not going to always be around to cater to your wife; she needs to respond to other people."

Judge, agitated and mumbling, walks away in the direction of his wife. "You better pray for your sake that Miles agrees to take care of you two extra days, or… you're out of here." Judge meets Miles in the courtyard to play a game of scrabble. "Miles, I am glad that you are here. I have to ask a huge favor of you."

"What's up?"

"I need you to pick up a couple of extra days with Mrs. Chapman."

"Well, I would love to help out but unfortunately, I've decided to cut back my hours at the health center. I'm going to take your advice and go to grad school."

"That's great, what's your major?"

"Law!"

"Maybe, just maybe, we can help each other out. How about I give you an offer you can't refuse."

"Sure…What's the offer?"

"I will pay your tuition and you can continue to work with Mrs. Chapman."

"Yeah right! My tuition is thirty thousand dollars." Judge reaches in his pocket and writes a check for thirty thousand dollars.

"I can't take this, I appreciate it but I can't take it."

"Oh, yes you can. I'm not giving it to you; young man, you will be earning it. I appreciate everything that you do for us. You are the only person that my wife responds to. Before coming here, she wouldn't even talk to me. She resents the hell out of me. You give her life and I love you for that."

"I'm speechless. Thanks sir, you know I love the two of you like my parents. I noticed the administrator speaking with you as I approached. Was it about Mrs. Chapman? What will happen to her if I don't take care of her?"

"The administrator is threatening to discharge her from the facility."

"Well we can't have that. I'm going to visit her now. Miles goes to the health care unit to visit Mrs. Chapman. Mrs. Chapman is busy drawing at her easel. "Good morning beautiful; how are you?" Mrs. Chapman smiles as Miles kisses her on the cheek.

"Hey, how about I take my best friend out for a drive today. I have some errands to run and you can accompany me. How about it? Mrs. Chapman grabs her coat and walks with Miles. While driving, Miles passes Mrs. Chapman an article with a picture of his biological parents. Mrs. Chapman begins to cough and sweat. She's turning red and jittery.

"Mrs. Chapman are you okay? What's wrong?" Miles pulls over. Mrs. Chapman tries to get out of the car but Miles stops her. Mrs. Chapman starts hollering, "This can't be true; this can't be true."

"What are you talking about Mrs. Chapman?" "Just take me home. Please take me home and promise me that you're not going to tell Judge about this article." With a loud scream, "Promise me!"

"Okay, okay, I promise that I won't mention it to Judge." Miles gives her a comforting hug then they drive away in silence. Kyla is running in the building. She's late for work. She looks as if she just jumped out of bed. Judge's two nosey neighbors notice her running down the hall. They both turn their noses up to her. When Kyla reaches her locker, she notices a dozen of roses sitting on her cleaning cart. She picks the card and smiles, "Sorry you got dumped on yesterday." She smells the roses and becomes very emotional. Her boss walks by and interrupts the moment.

"You're late again, and it's time for work." Kyla takes another smell of her roses, grabs her IPod and heads to the courtyard to work. Kyla is dancing as she sweeps the courtyard. She feels a deep stare on her body. When she looks up, Judge is smiling down on her from the huge archway. "Thank you," she whispers. Judge winks at her and walks away. Kyla hears her cell phone ringing. She drops her broom while trying to answer the telephone. "Hello."

"Hi Precious, how are you?"

"I asked you not to call me while I'm working. What do you want? I told you I would call you when something happens."

"Come on, I know you made something happen by now." Suspiciously, Kyla looks around to see and assure no one is listening or watching. "I think he likes me. I've been in his apartment."

"Bastard."

"Nothing happened; I'm scheduled to clean his apartment this week."

"Well…unfortunately, all emotions aside, you have a

job to do and I trust…umm…know…you are very good at your job." The phone now has a dial tone. John Jr. hung the phone up. Later that day, Kyla changes her clothes and proceeds to Judge's apartment. Judge opens the door with a smile. "Thank you for the flowers."

"You're quite welcome. That was my wife that dumped the food on you."

"I was wondering why you sent the flowers."

"I also would like to make it up to you by taking you to dinner."

"That's nice of you, but the flowers are enough."

"Come on; let this old man have some pleasure. We can go right now".

"I can't go to dinner like this; I need a change of clothes." Judge reaches in his pocket and pulls out his Platinum American Express Card.

"I know you do not expect me to walk in that mall with this card." She starts to laugh and speaks in a southern Negro slang, "Don't no black folks like me, own no Platinum American Express Card."

Judge smiles, "I have African American friends with more money than me. But, if it will make you feel better, here's some cash to get you something nice."

"Thank you, this is much better." Kyla walks towards the door. Judge stands back jiggling keys.

"Thanks again. The mall is kind of far to be walking." Kyla takes the keys.

"Would you like to know what vehicle you are driving?"

"Sure."

"It's a silver Bentley."

"A silver what? You mean an Allen Iverson Silver Bentley."

"Yes, if that's what you want to call it."

"You're really trying to get me arrested."

Kyla hands him the keys, "Do you have another car? Like a squatter."

"A what?"

"A hoopty?"

Judge is dumb founded. "I don't quite understand what you're saying. Would a Toyota do? Here's the key."

"Thanks again."

While Kyla is fiddling with the radio, Mrs. Chapman notices her driving by. Mrs. Chapman is startled to see this young beauty driving her husband's car. When Kyla reaches the mall, she's immediately greeted by two of her old partners in crime. "Hey what's up girl?"

"Nothing, what's up with you two?"

"You know us; we're still getting money. Are you trying to get down?"

"Nah, I'm cool. I'm clean from the game. I've been flying straight for a while now."

"You…flying straight? Did you hit the lottery or something?"

"Shelly, show her your knot, I bet you that would change her mind." Shelly pulls out a wade of money. Kyla laughs, "Y'all be careful, I'm out of here."

"When you come to your senses, you know where to find us. We're making a bet on how long this so called clean life of yours is going to last." Kyla smiles and walks a way. She finds a very sexy outfit from Macys. When Kyla returns back to the apartment, Judge is sitting on the sofa watching a movie. "Is it okay if I take a quick shower and freshen up?"

"You most certainly can." Kyla showers, gets dressed and is ready for excitement. "You look beautiful."

"Thank you." Kyla tosses Judge a bag. "Open it up, I bought you something too."

"You didn't have to buy me anything, I have plenty of clothes."

"Well since we're hanging out tonight, I don't want you looking like an old man."

Judge laughs, "Well if you hadn't notice, I am an old man."

"Well not tonight. Tonight, you are as young as you feel. How about that?" Kyla grabs his hand and heads towards the door. Judges opens the door to his beautiful silver Bentley. Kyla is mesmerized. She's touching the buttery soft leather seats and the computerized radio system. "What do you have a taste for?"

"Surprise me; I'm getting full off of this beauty here." She continues to rub the fixings.

"Have you ever been to Philadelphia?"

"Yes, I was in a few foster homes in the City of Brotherly Love."

"A few?"

"Yes a few. I'll talk to you about it someday." Judge pulls in front of Ruth Chris' Steak House. Kyla is let out of the car by a valet attendant. There is an opera show taking place next to the restaurant. The streets are crowded and people are everywhere. As they walk in the restaurant, an older white couple is coming out of the restaurant. "He looks old enough to be her grandfather and she looks like a tramp."

"Who cares? She looks good to me?"

"He must be rich to have a beautiful girl like that with him." Kyla and Judge start to laugh. They are having a great time in the dimmed atmosphere. "Tell me a secret."

"There's no big secret to my life. I do what I know

how to do in order to survive."

"That's not a secret."

"Well, since we have all night, I will tell you just a little bit about my life. I've been in twelve different foster homes. I was sexually molested at the age of nine and I've been beaten in almost all of the homes. Now that's my deep secret."

"Are you serious?"

"I'm serious as a heart attack."

"Where are your parents?"

"I don't know. I heard rumors that I was a trick baby. My mother was on crack."

"I'm sorry to hear that. I admire your strength."

"Now that you know all of this, are you still going to pursue me? And why are you pursuing me anyway?"

"Yes, I will continue to pursue you and to answer your next question, you've seen my wife. She doesn't know if she's coming or going. She's just too sick and I'm too lonely."

"I've always heard that marriage was for better or worst."

"Yes, you heard right, but sometimes better or worse can turn into bitter and boring."

"That still doesn't answer my question. Why me? There are plenty of rich single females in your community."

"Here's my secret. I'm attracted to young, sexy women of color." He raises his glass and they toast. "To finish off my answer, I think you are very interesting and special." She points to her arm where Special "K" is tattooed." "That's why they call me special "K".

10

Mrs. Chapman is awake at the nursing station. "Mrs. Chapman are you okay?" She nods her head up and down. "I saw something that I wish I wouldn't have seen today."

"Do you want to talk about it or would you like for me to call your husband?"

"No do not call him, I'll be okay. My son is on his way. I would like to talk to Miles." The nurse picks up the telephone to call Miles. Miles does not answer so she leaves a message. The two nurses are becoming worried about Mrs. Chapman.

"I've never heard her talk this much; she must really be worried about something."

"Did you know that Miles is the only staff person that she will talk to? She's very prejudice."

"Miles looks as if he's white, she probably doesn't know the difference and he sure doesn't know what color he is. I call him an Oreo." They both began to laugh.

Miles is rushing to get dressed so he can visit Kevin. He ignores the blinking light from his message box. He arrives at the prison early in order to have the full time with his father. Kevin is very excited to see Miles. He hugs Miles as soon as he is un-cuffed.

"How are you man?"

"I'm quite well. God is always good and always working in my life."

"So you're a Christian. huh?"

"I sure am. What about you."

"I believe in God."

"That's good. I want to talk to you about something."

"I'm all yours for the next hour."

"I have to be honest with you. I'm not sure if I'm your father or not. Your mother turned a lot of tricks during her addiction."

"Do I look like her?"

"Yes you do, except that she was about ten shades darker than you." They both laugh.

"What sort of men did she sleep with? Even more importantly, who were they?"

"Majority of them were upper class white men. A few of them may have been wealthy. They never used their real names." They continue to talk until the hour was up. They were so engrossed into their conversation the time escaped both of them. The alarm sounded and the big brawny correction officer signaled that their reunion was over.

As Miles left the prison and drove back to work, he pondered the conversation he held with Kevin. He did not know what to make of it. His emotions were mixed up; there was relief in finally knowing of his past but at the same time, sorrow for confronting the truth. Miles stops by the healthcare unit to visit with Mrs. Chapman. Her room is cold and empty. "Hey Amy, have you seen Mrs. Chapman?"

Amy is very sad. "Hello Miles, Mrs. Chapman passed away early this morning."

"What did you just say? What are you talking about?

What Happened?"

"Oh my gosh…You haven't been told. We tried to contact you. I'm so very sorry. Apparently, she over dosed on some medication that she was hoarding. I'm sorry Miles." Miles worked to compose himself. He did not quite understand what transpired from the time he dropped her off. Tears began to fall; his body began to shake. He attempts to contact Judge on his cell phone but he doesn't get an answer.

Judge is very confused and baffled. He stares at Mrs. Chapman's portrait. Although he was never truly in love with her, he did love what she added to his life. She gave him a sense of belonging. She accepted him with all of his faults, secrets, misdealing, and infidelities. She was loyal to him and to the end. She died with his deep dark secret inside of her. He never could understand her loyalty; you could not buy this type of loyalty. Judge hesitantly picks up the telephone to speak with Kyla. "Hello Kyla how are you?"

"I'm fine; I was just thinking about you, I had a great time last night. Thank you."

"I enjoyed myself too." Judge takes a deep breath.

"Are you okay?"

"My wife died last night."

"I'm so sorry. Is there anything I can do for you?"

"Well I don't feel like being alone tonight, Can you come over?" There's a silence on the line.

"Yes, I'll be over shortly."

"Is that a promise?"

"I've learned a long time ago not to make promises. My word is bond."

"Thanks, I'll see you shortly."

When I arrived at Judge's apartment, of course those

two old nosey bags were lingering around, whispering as usual. I decided to grab some Chinese food for dinner. My hands were full, with the food and my overnight bag as I approached Judge's apartment. As usual, the two old biddy-bodies were maintaining watch. I stared at the two of them as if to say, "Get a life." I was getting tired of letting them think that they were intimidating me. Judge greeted me with a warm hug. His apartment was in a mess. He had papers everywhere. I cleared up as much as I could, then I set the table for dinner. He was very grateful for the meal, but he told me at least three times that I didn't have to pick up the food and he would pay me back. I reassured him that it wasn't my last dollar and that I wasn't going to be homeless after spending twenty dollars for dinner. As solemn as the evening was, we managed to conjure up a few laughs as we watched *Why Did I Get Married.* Time flew by. It was 12:00a.m. and I decided it was time for me to leave. "Well the night has been fun; it's time for me to go." I wanted to see if he would ask me stay.

"Please stay, it's too late for you to travel home by yourself."

Although my body was sending mixed signals, I knew it would be inappropriate. He was well aware of my uneasiness with the situation. "I know what you must be thinking; this old man wants to take me to bed. Please understand that is not the case. I truly only want your company tonight. There are two extra bedrooms. All you have to do is just choose one. Right now…I can use a friend. I will enjoy seeing a fresh, beautiful face in the early morning."

As awkward as the situation felt, I wanted to be there for him. He sat me back on the sofa and laid his head in my lap. I began to massage his temples, as he read me stories from the book titled, *The Secret.* At that very moment, I had flashbacks of Frankie reading to me from the bible; the only difference was *The Secret* did not incorporate God. As he continued to read, I fell asleep inspired and motivated.

Judge carried me into the guest bedroom and kissed me good night. The night passed by as quickly as the evening; before I knew it, it was morning. I'm an early riser. The aroma from my soul cooking awakened Judge. "Something smells great, where did you learn to cook like that?"

"I'm a survivor, there's not much that I can't do."

"You're just a baby, how much surviving did your life call for?"

"Were you not listening to me the other night? Not only am I a survivor, I'm probably smarter than you are."

Judge lets out a burst of laughter. "Let's not get carried away."

"Okay, maybe I'm exaggerating a little, but I almost busted a perfect score on the pre-SAT, and I was only thirteen."

"That's great, why didn't you continue your education?"

"School was not a priority for me, besides I found it boring. I was always the first to finish my assignments then I would find myself acting out from boredom."

"You don't look like the type that started trouble."

"I didn't; trouble always found me. I was known as the dirty girl who wore hand-me-down clothes and ripped up sneakers; so the kids in school would tease me, which would provoke me to fight."

Judge listens with great intensity and concern. "Did you have any positive role models in your childhood?"

"Yeah, when I was in the eighth grade, my English teacher took a liking to me. After she was amazed by my pre-SAT scores, she kind of took me under her wing. She knew my living conditions were horrible, so she suggested that I stay with her until she found me a better home."

"That was pretty noble of her. Did she help you?"

"It was going great until one night she climbed into bed with me and tried to molest me."

"What did you do?"

"I whipped her ass. She pressed charges against me and I've been in the judicial system every since." I let out a deep sigh. "Now may I bless the food so you can taste what I'm made of?"

Judge nods his head in agreement then blurts out, "What do you want to do with your life?"

"Well…One day, I would like to go to college and study psychology; maybe add a few years of med school leading me up to a degree in psychiatry. Most importantly, I need to rebuild my relationship with my daughter; therefore, I want to obtain or shall I say, regain custody."

"Who has custody of her now?"

"Her father and his wife. Don't misunderstand me; they're good to her. I get to see her on Wednesdays and every other weekend. She loves going to church, so she forces me to church on Sundays."

Enough of me; enjoy your food."

"What about your job here? I don't want to be the reason you become unemployed."

"Oh, you don't have to worry about that. I requested a few days off. Anyways, I can just as well get another job. Have you made arrangements yet for your wife?"

"Yeah…We made sure that we planned ahead just in case."

"Oh! What about your children?"

"They've been properly notified. Things have been taken care of."

Unplanned, Kyla spent the entire day with Judge. Everyone and everything are oblivious to their presence. After dinner, Kyla is sitting on the sofa watching television. "Hey what are you watching?"

"Jeopardy, let's play."

"No one can beat me at Jeopardy."

"Put your money where your mouth is, ladies first." Kyla misses the first question and they both laugh. Judge answers the next question. Kyla stutters and misses the next question.

"Try again," Kyla shouts, "Jupiter."

"Wrong!" Judge laughs as Kyla becomes frustrated.

"I quit."

"No, you are not quitting, it's only a game, besides I thought you were a fighter."

"I am."

"Well let's play. You challenged me, so I'll say when it's over. You're coming up with some great answers. All you have to do is think a little harder and become a little smarter."

"I don't feel like thinking smarter, harder, whatever you're saying."

"How about this, if you get the next four answers correct, I'll give you these." Judge reaches in his pocket and dangles a set of keys.

"What do they belong to?"

"My gold Honda."

"Are you serious?"

"I wouldn't lie to you, so start thinking." Judge puts the keys on the table. Kyla answers the next four questions correctly without hesitation. She picks up the keys, grabs Judge's arm and starts to dance. "I told you that you can do it. You just need incentives and someone to believe in you."

"What everrrrrr…you're out of a car." Judge walks over to the radio and changes the station. He puts on smooth R&B. Kyla changes the station. The song *Electric Slide* is playing on the radio.

"I'm going to show you how to line dance. This is one of the easiest dances for white people to do." Judge is laughing while trampling over Kyla's feet. "Okay, we'll go back to your station." A beautiful song by Celine Dionne is sounding from the radio. Kyla lays her head on Judge's chest as they dance. Kyla and Judge's dance is interrupted by the ringing of her cell phone. A strong hard voice is on the other end. "Meet me at the Blue Parrot at 8:00 sharp. Rattled by the call and the command, Kyla hangs up the telephone. "It has been fun, but I have an emergency. I have to go."

"Is everything okay?" "

Yes, I'll call you in an hour." I refreshed my makeup as I hurried down the hall. When I arrived at the Blue Parrot, John Jr. was sitting just as handsome as ever under the tropical lighting. "You're late". He reaches over to kiss me, but I pulled back. "What is it? I told you that I would contact you."

"Are you falling in love with my daddy?" I hear the two of you have been hanging out."

"Screw you; you said no one was going to get hurt. Did you kill your own mother?"

"She asked me to," Emotionlessly he exclaimed as he puffed on his cigar.

"You are a ruthless bastard."

"Oh relax, She just found out that she had brain cancer. Why would I want my poor mother to suffer? That bastard that you're running around with made her suffer enough. Besides, now you can persuade him into marrying you."

"That was not part of the deal. You don't care about anybody but yourself. You selfish, inconsiderate bastard! I figured that you had something to do with your mother's death. I just knew it."

"You're not here to figure out things...Remember, you have a job to do. I want what belong to me. Then you can go back to your so called clean life." John Jr. laughs hysterically.

"I don't know nor do I care about the personal issue you have with your father. All I know is that Judge is a changed man now. I have him opening up to me. He is not the same man that he used to be."

"I guess you think that you're not the same whore that you use to be. Remember, you work for me and don't forget that." He grabs me closer to him. "I put you there because I knew he would fall for you. My mother's casket hasn't been selected or arrangements settled and already he's falling in love with you. Huh...and you say that he's a changed man. Huh, he's the same self-centered bastard that he's always been and he's going to pay for driving my mother crazy. Not to mention the neglect that he showed to my brother and me." He starts to caress my hair and I yanked away. "All this wouldn't be if he wasn't a nigger lover."

"Listen at the pot calling the kettle black. If I recall, I believe that you were in love with me first." I slung my hair in his face and turned away.

A sweet whisper covered the air, "I'm still in love with you, but...business is business." John Jr. reaches in his brief case and pulls out documents. "Here are the documents to your future. The only thing they require is my signature. That's all I have to do is just sign on the dotted line and your probation will be erased; then and only then, can you apply for custody. So do what you were hired to do."

I took a deep breath then walked away.

11

Miles is sitting in his room puzzled and dis-traught about the ripped sketching pad that he found in Mrs. Chapman's room. "Why would Judge rip this page out? What was she hiding? Better yet, what did she know? I have to find this paper." He reminisces about the story that one of his co- workers told him. He found this story very hard to believe about Judge. Miles has always placed

Judge above all others. As far as he was concerned, neither Judge nor Mrs. Chapman could do any wrong. Judge and his wife have been nothing but good to Miles. On the other hand, the rumor was that Judge had an affair with a young black girl who held a job as a certified nursing assistant. It was a secret affair that lasted approximately a year. Judge bought her furniture and very expensive gifts in return for her sexual favors. Up until that point, things were going well for the both of them until her live-in boyfriend found out about the affair; afterwards, she had to make the decision to break it off with Judge. Judge was starting to catch feelings or his ego got in the way. His personality did not accept too kindly to losing; anything or anyone. The routine was that the young lady would receive a weekly allowance from Judge. On this particular day, the Judge made other arrangements for the young lady to retrieve her allowance. He made plans to be unavailable and instructed her to the whereabouts of the funds. She was to retrieve it from his favorite suit jacket. Unbeknownst to her, the Judge had decided that if he was going to lose; she would too. He made a formal complaint that moneys were being stolen from his residence. The administration staff installed a security camera to catch the perpetrator. The young lady was caught going into Judge's closet, searching his pockets, and walking away with a few hundred dollars. Needless to say, she lost her license and her job. The facility even pressed charges against her. Embarrassed by the predicament, she didn't tell too many people the truth for fear that her boyfriend would become privy to the information.

Miles perplexed by the many different rumors wanted to get to the bottom. He needed to know the truth. He called Judge and asked if he could meet him at the courtyard as soon as possible. The past two weeks have been rather disturbing to Miles. Never before has he ever been so confused. He did not want to think or believe that he was fooled by two people; nor did he want to believe that he was naïve. He knew the answer lied somewhere in the apartment. He needed access. Giving Judge enough time to make it to the courtyard, Miles managed to avoid bumping into him and quickly advanced to the apartment. Miles has always had a key to it and unlocked the door. In he went, like a thief moving in the night. Feverously, he searched Judge's suite jackets. He knew there was not much time and the man did have a lot of suits. Finally, he reached in a pocket and pulled out a slip of paper. The paper had a picture of a white man choking a black lady. The picture was rather crewed and infantile. "Why would she draw a picture of a white man choking a black lady?" The background of the picture is full of dirt and filth.

Miles mumbles to himself, "Why would Judge want this picture?" He put every item back in place, restored Judge's closet to normal, secured the drawing in his pocket, and headed to the courtyard to meet Judge.

"Hello Miles, what took you so long? You're never late."

"I'm sorry; I just can't seem to get it together since the death of your wife. I've been on edge lately."

"What's the urgency? You sounded desperate on the telephone."

"Well I didn't mean to sound so anxious, but I wanted to talk about Mrs. Chapman's death. I can't stop thinking about her."

"I know it's hard for you; the two of you were pretty close. I know she's smiling down on you especially if God is who you say He is."

"Thanks Judge, I needed to hear that." Miles finishes his afternoon with Judge and races home. He phones Judge's youngest son Sean. "Hi Sean this is Miles, I would like to talk to you about something. When can we meet?"

"I'm free tonight. I'm in Rehoboth now. I can meet you at the Riverfront at 8:00p.m."

"That's a bet; I'll see you at Kahunaville. Miles heads towards the waterfront early. Kahunavilles is having a beach party. The music is blasting and people are dancing and prancing in their bathing attire. Miles gets a tap on his shoulder. "Hey! Don't I know you?" Miles is startled when he turns around. "Yeah, you're the helpful lady from Crozer Hospital. How are you?"

"I'm great."

You look totally different today."

"I was at work; now I'm at play."

"Nice swim wear."

"Thank you." She gives Miles a seductive smile. "Why didn't you call me?"

"What are you drinking?"

"You should never answer a question with a question." Laughter filled the air. "I'm drinking Apple Martinis."

Miles raises his hand to get the bartender's attention. "Can you give this pretty lady an apple martini? And I don't have an excuse why I didn't call you but can I make it up to you?" They toast in agreement. While Miles and the pretty receptionist are busting it up, Sean spots Miles from across the bar. "Hey Miles, what's up man?" "You got it." They give each other a brotherly embrace then Miles introduces Sean to Angela.

"Well Miles, it looks like you two have a lot of catching up to do. Give me a call when you can. By the way, thanks for drink."

"You're quite welcomed." She struts away with her savvy walk. Miles looks at Sean and smiles. "Is that your girlfriend? She's hot."

"No I met her a few weeks ago."

"I'm sorry I was so short with you at my mother's funeral; you know I can't stand the sight of that man too long. He makes my skin crawl."

"I've noticed that. That's what I want to talk about. Why do you hate your father so much?"

"He's more of a father to you than he's ever been to me or my brother. He's always showed more love toward the outside world. He treated the trash man better than he treated us."

"I find that so hard to believe."

"How long have you known my parents?"

"Umm…about five or six years."

"How often does he speak of my brother or me?" Miles

is completely silent. "I thought so, never. One thing is for certain, he's still the same selfish, useless bastard that's he's always been. When we were younger, Judge would walk in the house and wouldn't even say hello to us, this includes my mother too. He never answered her when she would talk to him. What's for dinner? Who called for me? Did you take my clothes to the dry cleaners? Those are the only words we heard from him. My mother lived as if she was always on trial. He was an evil man and I've always believed that he had some sort of mental or emotional disorder. Maybe even bipolar. His moods would change by the hour. I'll never forget how he would drive my brother and me to our soccer games and not say a word to us. As soon as our feet hit the soccer field, he was the proud father. He would greet the other children with smiles and magic tricks. He greeted the other adults with 'Ma'am and Sir.' He talked to everyone except us." Sean puts his chin in his chest and became very silent.

"Are you okay Sean?"

"I'm fine. Did I mention the numerous affairs he had?"

"No."

"Oh yeah, and they were all with under privileged minority women. He chose women with legal charges against them or who was on probation. He did this for control."

"Tell me more about these women."

"I don't know much about them. My uncle later filled us in about these affairs. His passion for colored women doesn't bother me. I was bothered by his cowardice. He did not know how to be real. He constantly played the game *Truth or Consequences.* Every day we were in search of the real John Chapman. We never really found him and instead the three of us suffered."

"Can you give me any supported facts about his practice? Location? Personnel? Anything would do!

"All that I know is that he was working in Philadelphia. By the way, what's it to you? Do you know something that I need or should know?"

"Today, I am not sure of anything. I just need to get to the bottom of some unanswered questions. You know man…I loved your mother. She was like a second mother to me. Her death is just disturbing. I just can't put my finger on it. Anyway, I am truly grateful for your help. Thanks man."

"Anytime. By the way, you're the son that he's always wanted. Keep in touch." They embrace and say their good byes."

12

Miles walks into the Philadelphia Library. He doesn't know where to begin. "Hello sir, may I help you?" "Yes ma'am, I'm trying to find the criminal court case that was trialed under a certain Judge. "Well, if you have the case information, docket number, or the like, you can check in the legal section. It may be quicker to access the information online. It's considered public record; therefore granting anyone access. "Thanks ma'am. You have been most helpful." Miles climbed the stairs to the legal section of the library. There were shelves and more shelves of books. After contemplating the task at hand, he decided that he could get the information he was seeking elsewhere.

Miles decided that he would pay Kevin a visit. He thought that maybe Kevin would be able to give him a few more details into his mother's death. He had pieces of the puzzle but they were not connecting as of yet. As always, Kevin is delighted to have Miles' company. They exchange embraces and sat down.

"Miles, I look forward to our visits. Would you believe that you are the only person I've spoken to outside of this place since I've been here?"

"Why is that?"

"I don't have much family and the ones I do have

given up on me a long time ago. But on a better note, I'm up for parole soon."

"That's great news. I am hearing reluctance in your voice. You don't sound too excited."

"I've been here half my life. This is all I know. I'm excited because when I get out I'll get to go to a church and worship. That's all I have to look forward to."

"A few weeks ago, you could say that; but today, you have me. I'll help you get a job. I have a friend who's a Judge and he knows a lot of people. I'm sure he can help you. His name is Judge Chapman. Does that name sound familiar to you?"

"I'm not sure. Did he practice in Philadelphia?" Miles asks with excitement.

"The name sounds very familiar. I'm certain I have heard it before and he did practice in Philadelphia."

"Did my mother know him?"

"Most of the men she solicited didn't give a first name, and I barely got to see them. There were two of them who wanted me to either watch or listen." Miles closes his eyes in shame. "Forgive me man, I was sick. I was addicted to that poison. Every day when I pray I ask your mother for forgiveness."

"I'm sure she's forgiven you. Don't keep beating yourself up."

"Well on another note, one of my former buddies is here on a petty theft charge. He told me that your twin sister is alive and she resides in the Delaware County area. Unfortunately, she didn't turn out as well; I hear that she's a street hustler. See if you can find her, she might need your help."

"My plate is full, but I'm curious to meet her. After all, she is my twin."

"I hope when you find out all of the information that you need, that you will continue to visit me."

"I sure will. I enjoy our talks and I look forward to them."

As before, the time races by quickly. The guard walks over to their table. Kevin and Miles shake hands and Kevin is handcuffed and escorted back to his cell. Miles is driving around in Chester, Pa. He pulls up to the old men on the bench. There are beer cans and empty bottles on the ground. Miles is generous enough to pick up the trash. One of the men shouts out, "Oh you're back again, huh! You just can't get enough of this place. It is clearly evident that you are not from here. You are picking up the trash those bad ass kids threw over there." Miles lets out a big laugh. "I'm looking for a young lady who might be Kevin and Tracy's daughter." The other man shouts out,

"You're talking about Kyla. We thought you were looking for her the first time you came around here. "You're not the only one looking for her. A young white man was riding around here asking questions about her." The other man adds his two cents. "She's an old slickster; a beautiful girl no doubt, but she's bad. We don't see much of her anymore. We heard she has a daughter who lives across town. That's a nice boy she had that baby for. He owns the gas station up the hill. Maybe he can help you find her."

"Thanks a lot old heads. Here's twenty dollars, treat yourselves to some coffee."

"Thanks for the twenty, but we sure won't be buying any coffee. We are going to get us a real drink." They all burst into laughter. Miles is curious as he cruise the road looking for the gas station that the older men directed him to. Miles pulls into the first gas station that he sees. He is greeted by an intelligent looking gentleman. "Hey what's up man? How can I help you?"

"My name is Miles. This is going to sound really weird, but I'm looking for a young lady by the name of Kyla."

"Look man if she burnt you, all I can tell you is to press charges. I'm not paying anymore of her debts."

"No she doesn't owe me anything. I believe that she's my sister."

"Sister! Kyla doesn't have any brothers or sisters; as a matter of fact, she's an orphan. She has no one."

"We were separated at an early age and she knows nothing about me. Where can I find her?" Miles reaches in his pocket. "Look here's our birth certificate."

Taron reads the birth certificate. He looks at Miles for a few seconds. "Man your guess is as good as mine. The last I saw her she was doing okay. She had a job and supposedly, abandoned the hustle game."

"Is she on drugs?"

"No way man; she has never touched the stuff. She's petrified of drugs. Her addiction has never been a substance; she just loves the hustle and bustle."

"Who are you to her?"

"I'm sorry man, my name is Taron. We have a beautiful daughter together."

"Were the two of you ever married?"

"No she wasn't ready when I proposed to her. I tried to give her a better life but it wasn't enough. She's by far the smartest girl I know. Anything she tries to do, she masters it except falling in love." Taron points to the picture on his glass counter top. "Here's a picture of Sky, This is my angel."

"She's beautiful."

"Wait until you see her mother. You'll see where she

gets her looks from. Kyla can have the world if she puts her mind to it."

"Can I give you a telephone number to give to her?"

"Sure and good luck finding her."

"Thanks man." Miles and Taron shake hands.

Miles goes to Hockessin Hills. The maintenance crew is cleaning out Mrs. Chapman's room. Miles becomes very sentimental. He walks in the room full of grief. "Hey man can I have a few minutes alone in here?" "You sure can." The maintenance crew leaves Miles alone in the room. Miles walks around the room starring; he begins to talk to himself. "Mrs. Chapman, I know you want to tell me something, but what is it?" Before he could finish his sentence, a wind blows and knocks everything off of her table except her floral sketching book. Miles is startled. He picks up the book and flips the pages slowly. Mrs. Chapman wrote a short summary on each sketching. Miles is distracted by a torn page. He dials Judge. "Hello Judge, how are you?"

"I'm fine; thanks. How are you?"

"I'm cool."

"Well I'm on my way out of town and my flight leaves at 6:00pm."

"Where are you headed?"

"I'm going to the islands with a friend of mine. Can you feed my fish for me? I'll be back in three weeks."

"Sure I'll feed your fish and be safe."

"I'll leave my itinerary and some cash for you with the concierge if you need it." After 6:00, Miles immediately goes to Judge's apartment. He rambles through Judge's things. "Why can't I find anything?" He stops rambling through the cabinets and runs to Judge's closet. He checks each suit jacket until he finds a little scrapbook. He smiles as he turns the pages and reminisces about Mrs. Chapman. While turning the pages, he finds a letter addressed to him. It reads:

Dear Miles, You gave me hope and laughter. I never hated people of color. I just envied them. Of all the ways I tried to please Judge, I knew I could never totally satisfy him because of the color of my skin. You showed me that skin is only color and love is much deeper than the flesh. I hope you continue to care for Judge the same as you cared for me. He needs you and he owes you.

Miles became puzzled by the letter; especially the ending. He continues to turn the pages. *The front of my past.* This is an interesting title. "Miles continues to read. Whoever shall hold this letter, let the truth be told.

This story is going back almost twenty-five years ago. Judge Chapman and Rob were best friends. At this time, Rob was running for the mayor of Philadelphia. They were two well respected men with the same interest, a passion for women of color. For some reason, they both pursued these women who were caught up in the criminal justice system. One day, a story came across the news that told of a murder that had taken place in a hotel on 13th and Spruce. The news reporter reported that a man had murdered his wife because they had a fight over drugs. Judge walked into the kitchen in the middle of the story and he froze in his tracks. I said to him, "It's really a shame how that man killed his wife. She was the mother of his twins." Later, Judge would slip and make a big mistake. Coincidentally, the case was trialed in Judge's courtroom. The poor guy couldn't afford a lawyer, so Rob and Judge were responsible for him receiving the worst public defender in the Pennsylvania's system.

The guilt or knowing this and doing nothing about it has haunted me my entire life. He and Rob will one day pay in hell for what they did.

Miles starts to scream. He is hysterical. He's jumping up and down in a rage. "No, I can't believe this, this can't be real." Miles is so upset; he cries all the way home. He runs straight to his bedroom; retrieves his messages from his answering machine. While he sits there holding his head and deleting unwanted messages, he pauses when he hears the sixth message, "Hello Miles, My name is Kyla. Taron told me that you were looking for me. I hear that I'm your twin sister. I can't wait to meet with you. Unfortunately, I'm going out of town for a couple of weeks, but I will give you a call as soon as I return. I can't wait to meet you." Miles rewinds the message over and over again. "This voice sounds familiar." He looks at the caller ID box. The box reads Judge William Chapman. He grabs his head and paces the floor. "Special "K" can't be the one. She can't be my sister. Miles runs outside, jumps in his Jeep, and quickly drives away. He's constantly looking at the clock. He drives to the Philadelphia airport. He goes to the check-desks at all of the international flights. He calls Sean from his cell phone. The phone continues to ring. Miles leaves a message. "Hi Sean, this is Miles. Please give me a call as soon as possible." He calls John Jr. The answering machine comes on. He leaves a message for John Jr. to call him back. Miles is unsuccessful with finding Judge and Kyla. Miles is starting to panic. He calls the concierge at Judge's apartment building. "Hello Sir, this is Miles, I'm the gentleman that takes care of Judge Chapman's fish when he's away. He left a copy of his itinerary at the desk for me. Is it okay if I come by and pick it up?" "Sure I don't see why not." While Miles is driving to pick up the itinerary, his cell phone rings. He answers with intensity, "Hello!"

"Hey Miles what's up?"

Miles is screaming, "Your dad is a deceiving murderer and he's with my sister as we speak." There was a lull in the air. John Jr. is shocked.

"Your sister, who are you talking about and why did you call my dad a murderer?"

"It's a long story and I have to go. I'm taking the next flight out. I'll give you a call when I get back." Miles slams the telephone down. He races home because he knew what had to be done. He's sweating and jittery as he packs a few things for his trip. Miles rushes toward the door. "Slow down son, are you okay? Why the rush to go out of town for a couple of days?"

"If you need to call me I can be reached on my cell phone. There are some things I have to take care of. Don't worry; I'll be home in a couple of days."

Miles' mom gives him a hug and a kiss. "Be careful and call us if you need us. Miles' father chimes in. "Take care son," Miles throws his bag in his Jeep and drives away. Miles is driving on the back roads to the airport. It's dark, dreary and drizzling. The roads are very slippery and leaves are scattered everywhere. He listens to Kirk Walum as he makes the proper adjustments to the rear view mirror. A pick up truck appears to be following him. He speeds up and the truck speeds up behind him. The high beam lights coming from the truck blinds his view behind him. Miles picks up speed while both vehicles are passing the speed limit. "Who the hell is this following me?" They drive up and down hills. The pick-up truck is trailing Miles at high speed. Miles reaches for his cell phone. He manages to dial 9-1- then he's bumped by the force of the pick up truck. He loses his phone; it flies to the back of his jeep. Miles continues to drive as fast as he can, while the truck continues to try to bump him off of the road. "What the hell do you want from me?" He yells out the window as he throws his truck in third gear as he quickly turns into Clear Creek Park. The pick up truck tries to turn but flips over and over and runs into a flock of deer. The truck is not moving. Miles stops ahead of the truck. He finds his cell phone and dials 9-1-1. He walks over to the truck and pulls the dead man's head off of the antler from a deer. "It's John Jr. What the hell was he chasing me for?" Miles is devastated to see John Jr. dead on the scene. When the police arrive at the scene, Miles gives his statement. He doesn't let the police officer know that he knows John Jr.

13

Kyla and Judge are overlooking the ocean in Puerto Vallatta, Mexico. His magnificent Villa sits on the highest hill in that area. Kyla runs from room to room like a kid in a candy store. She's jumping on the bed and posing in each mirror that she passes. "What room would you like to claim?"

"I like them all, let's see, we'll be here for two weeks, so that's enough time to sleep in all of the rooms at least twice." She kisses Judge on the cheek and gives him a big hug. "Thank you so much for bringing me here. This is just what I need, especially after getting fired."

"Why did you get fired?"

"They claim I was late too many times." Kyla is interrupted by the ringing sound of a doorbell. Kyla runs to the door.

She opens the door with a big smile. Judge introduces her to the staff that will be catering to her for the next two weeks. "Kyla, this is Aurelio, Maria, and Juan. You have your own personal chef, maid and chauffeur." Judge kisses Maria and shakes Aurelio and Juan's hand. "Whatever this beautiful lady wants, make sure that it's doubled."

"Si", says Aurelio. Judge reaches out for Kyla's hands and walks her out to the patio.

"This is so beautiful."

"It's time that you see the finer side to life. The world isn't as cold as you think it is." He hands her a box from Tiffany's Jewelry Company. "For whatever reason, you got dealt a bad hand; it's now time to change your hand."

"Why me?"

"Why not you?" I smiled then opened the box. With excitement, "Hey this is the bracelet that I saw in that magazine. How did you know I was admiring it?"

"You only look at it every time you come to my place." I gave him a friendly nudge. He puts the bracelet on my wrist and I kissed him again. "Thank you again. So what do I owe you for all of this?"

"I don't want anything that you don't want me to have. You don't owe me anything."

"Nobody ever did anything for me without me doing something for them."

"I just want to see you happy and watch you enjoy your life. Can you do that? You have the whole world right in front of you."

"I'm tired of living my life on the edge all of the time. You know what I really want to do."

"No, but I know that you're going to tell me."

"I really want to strengthen my walk with Christ. The only time I really find myself at peace is when I'm reading my bible. Do you know what it is to have a relationship with Him?"

"To be honest, I don't. I did something that I can't forgive myself for. It has haunted me every single day of my life. Because of my guilt, I avoid God because I know he would never forgive me."

"See, that's the beauty of God, he's not like man, he'll always forgive us. No one sin is greater than the next. Have you ever asked for forgiveness?"

“No I was always too ashamed to even talk about it with God.”

“Hey guess what? He’s God, He’s all knowing and all seeing. He’s ready for your repentance whenever you’re ready to submit. Know that all of your money or power cannot replace the feeling of true peace.” I ran in the villa and grabbed my bible. “Look at this, Matthew 6:10-15, *God is no respecter of persons what he did for one person, he’ll do for the next.* He’s a forgiving God. He forgave me.”

”How do I ask? I haven’t been in a church in over twenty years.”

“You don’t have to be at church or in front of a preacher to ask for forgiveness. Just ask him.”

“How do you know all of this?”

“Because God forgave me on a floor in a hotel bathroom. I was in Atlantic City and I picked this old women’s purse. Inside was an article about her three children who had gotten burnt in a fire. Apparently, she got blamed for their deaths because she left them home alone. She served a few years in prison for this.”

“How did this story save you?”

“On the back of the article was another story. She was homeless for two years. She lost her house and everything she owned when she went to prison. She started writing poetry for people on the boardwalk. Her story is amazing; she wrote a poem for this woman for ninety-nine cents. It just so happen that the woman she wrote the poem for worked for Hallmark greeting cards. Now the homeless woman is very successful. She also wrote how God saved her life and she’ll give up all of her wealth just to have those last minutes with her children. This was in her wallet.”

"Why are you crying?"

"I took the only thing she had left of her children. I took her pictures of them and this story. She stated that she read this article everyday just to keep her going. I took the only thing she had."

"Wow…why didn't you just mail the wallet back to her?"

"I had the wallet in my hand and I began to shiver after reading this story. I was so scared, I started crying and begging God for forgiveness. I told him that I was sorry for all of my sins and how I want to change my life. I thought about everything Frankie tried to teach me about God. I got in the bed only to be awakened a half an hour later with the worst pain in my life. This pain was worst than childbirth labor. I was calling my friend, who was in the other bed, but he couldn't hear me. I was lying on a cold marble floor butt naked squirming like a baby. No one could hear my cry. I know God was delivering me from all of my evilness. He was setting me free. So, I don't know what your past holds, but give it to God and you'll be all right." Judge grabbed me and kissed me on my forehead. "You never said what you did with the wallet." "I mailed it back to her with a note that said, "Thanks for being my angel! God is so good that he'll use anything or anybody." "I see."

Judge and I were having a great time on his yacht. We played scrabble and sipped tropical drinks all afternoon. I thought I was dreaming. Everything I asked for was handed to me. Judge even had his own private staff to cater to us. "Did I say thank you for bringing me here?" "Only a hundred times." We both laughed. On the other side of the water, Kevin was waiting for his hearing. He was sitting outside the courtroom reading and meditating on his favorite scripture. *(Habbaku 2:3 For the vision is yet for an appointed time, but at the end it shall speak, and not lie: though it tarry, wait for it; because it will surely come, it will not tarry.)*

When his name is called, he's greeted by three men sitting behind a wooden table. Although he's handcuffed, he walks in with confidence and grace. One of the men stares at Kevin over the top of his glasses. "So Mr. Johnson, you served twenty years and we don't have any complaints on record for you. How did you manage not to get in trouble at least one time?" "The grace of God, sir." "Are you telling us that you're reformed?" "Yes Sir. I repented to God and asked him to forgive me of my sins. With all respect, I served my time for the crime that I was charged with, and more importantly, God has set me free in the spiritual, now I need to be let free in the natural." The three men go in for a side bar. "Well Mr. Johnson, I hope you have a blessed and prosperous life. You are a free man."

Miles arrives at the Puerto Valletta, Airport. It's a very hot and muggy day. He grabs his luggage and walks through the airport in a hurry. Miles immediately jumps in a cab. "Can you take me to a hotel please?" Miles stares out of the window not concentrating on the beautiful sceneries. As soon as Miles checks into the hotel, he retrieves his messages from his cell phone. The first message is from Kevin. "Hey Miles. For the grace of God and the love of his mercy, I'm a free man. You're the first person that I thought of calling. Now that I think about it, you're the only person that I know to call. Give me a call when you can and I sincerely thank you for everything and...I love you man."Miles closes his eyes and thanks God. He is ecstatic. Miles is happy for Kevin, but he cannot lose his focus. He must find Kyla before it's too late. Miles immediately takes a cab to Judge's villa. When he arrives at the villa, he's fascinated with the structure. He lets himself through a sliding glass door. Miles helps himself to the television remote control and a bottle of beer. He's sitting in the chair channel surfacing and tapping his foot on the Italian marble floor. Judge and Kyla walks in the door laughing. She stops in her tracks when she notices Miles. "Hi, you look familiar, where do I know you from?" She grabs her bikini wrap as she eases back from Miles. "Hello, I'm Miles I work at Hockessin Hills." Judge shockingly interrupts, "Hi Miles, what brings you here unannounced?"

Judge is startled by the evil look on Mile's face. I began to feel the tension. "Would you guys like to be alone?"

Miles blurts out, "No. You need to stay right where you are." I moved closer to Judge. I was becoming very uneasy with this scene. I grabbed the Judge's arm. Miles face is furious. He pulls out a picture and thrust it in Judge's face. Judge looks at the picture then pulls himself a drink. "Judge what is that? What are you looking at?" Judge takes a sip of his drink.

"I didn't do it. I would never kill anyone." Miles throws the picture at him. "Explain it then. If you are so innocent, I'm sure you have a good explanation. This was my god damn mother, and my father did a life sentence because of a sick fetish that you have for black women."

I had to jump in. "What is he talking about?"

"Why not tell her? Tell her about your lust for women of color. Tell your black fantasy what I'm talking about. Everybody thinks you're so great. You sure did have me fooled." Judge looks at me with a blank stare. "Yes, Kyla I bet he has you fooled too. And by the way, I'm Miles, your twin brother."

Judge interrupts," Miles, can you please listen? I didn't

kill her. Yes, I was there, but I didn't lay a finger on her." Judge pauses, "What do you mean, you're her twin brother?"

"Don't you see the family resemblance? Yes…I'm your lover's twin. Later for that, how could you take advantage of a person's weakness for your pleasure?"

I could no longer listen to the accusations. I needed answers. I wanted answers. I jumped between the two of them and yelled, "I don't know what is going on, but someone please tell me what the hell you two are talking about."

Judge shouts, "If we can all sit down like adults, I can explain everything." We all sat on the sofa. Miles grabs another beer. I'm nervous and I catch myself biting my nails. Judge takes a deep breath. "I didn't kill anyone. Over twenty years ago, my friend Rob asked me to hang out with him one night just to have some fun." Miles interrupts him, "Kyla their idea of fun was to prostitute drug addicts."

"Can I please finish?" Well, it all went bad. Tracy who was the victim made the mistake of telling Rob that he was the father of her twins. When she told him that, he snapped and started choking her; he wouldn't stop. When I finally was able to unravel his fingers from around her neck it was too late." "Why did Mrs. Chapman think that you murdered her?"

"Because…I used my position and power to cover it all up for him. I made sure that I was the Judge to hear the case and that's when I sentenced Kevin, her husband, to twenty years in prison."

I could not believe what I was hearing. I began to shake my head. I was so confused. "This can't be true; this has to be a lie. Please Judge tell me that I'm dreaming."

"No, you're not dreaming Kyla; it's true. We were separated; after that, I was adopted and you weren't. I'm sorry."

I immediately put my face in the pillow. This was one of those moments in my life where I just didn't know what to do. I've always wanted to know who I was and where I came from, but I didn't expect it to surface this way. Frankie always told me to be careful what I ask for and what I pray for. He always expressed the importance of putting words out in the universe, he said, "What we put out and what we expect will happen, might not happen the way we want it to." I wish Frankie was here to help me out with this. I need him so much. I miss and I love him so much.

For the first time in my life I realize that I do need people. I just don't know what to do at this moment. Miles interrupts my thoughts, "The only reason I came here is to tell you so he wouldn't hurt you."

"I would never hurt you Kyla. Yes, I'm guilty, but I'm not a murderer. Miles you know that I love you as a son, and Kyla I have so much love for you. Can you both please forgive me?"

Miles and I were both silent. Miles stands with one hand on his hip and the other hand on the wall. I continued to rock back and forth in my chair confused as ever. "Com'on Kyla, let's go."

"How can I have fallen for a man who is partially responsible for my entire life? You are responsible for taking my parents away from me. I don't care if they were addicts or not. They were still my parents." My frustration was starting to boil. I charged towards Judge. Miles picked me up by the waist and carried me to the door. I continued to scream. "So you look at me as a trick too, huh! How could I think you were any different?" I commanded Miles to put me down. I walked in the room and gathered all my things. I put my entire luggage near the door. As I was turning the door knob, the reflection of my bracelet was radiating around the room. I snapped off the bracelet and handed it to Judge. "What a difference a day can make. I'm still a diamond in the rough." Judge did not extend his hand to except the bracelet.

"I bought that from my heart, you keep it." I laid the bracelet on the counter top. Judge grabbed my arm, "You just taught me a life lesson on forgiveness. Are you who you say you are?" Before I could answer, Miles interrupts.

"I thought you were different man. I thought you were actually one of the good guys." We both picked up my luggage and headed out the door. Miles and I had to be related because we were both very stubborn. As we were leaving, Judge offered us his chauffer to drive us to our destination. We both refused the ride. We traveled up the dusty highway carrying luggage. I had no idea just how heavy my luggage was; I was not physically fit for this. My adrenaline was high; my anger became my strength that I was able to keep up with Miles. It seemed as if we walked for miles before we found a restaurant. I was so glad to reach a civil environment. When we entered the restaurant, the Mira chi Band was playing. It was loud and the people seemed to be louder. Miles took the initiative to order for us. He ordered the both of us beer and chicken quesadillas. After I freshened up in the ladies room, I felt like myself again, "Hey thanks for the beer, but I'm a wine and tropical drink girl."

"I'm sorry; believe me it will not go to waste. Are you okay with the chicken quesadillas?"

"I love food, so I'm sure that I'll like it." After eating and drinking our drinks, we noticed that we were probably the only two English-speaking people in the restaurant.

"Hola, can you call a taxi for us?"

"No English, No English."

"Okay, Miles, it seems like it's going to be a long evening." We both laughed. Miles ordered another round of drinks for us. "Are you okay Kyla?"

"I'm fine. I'm just a little overwhelmed with all the surprises. I come from being a loner, to having a twin brother, a dead mother, and a white father."

Miles laughed. "I was just as shocked as you are. That's why I came to find you."

"I appreciate that. How do you feel about everything? You knew Judge longer than I did. I use to see you guys kicking it all of the time."

"Yeah, he was like a father to me. I'm shocked and hurt. A lot of pain is coming from this. I was too pissed off to tell him about my accident yesterday. Judge's oldest son died chasing me yesterday." I almost choked on my drink. My face was beginning to become flushed. "Repeat that. What did you say?" "Judge's oldest son John Jr. died chasing me in a car yesterday."

"Why was he chasing you?"

"I don't know. He was trying to bump me off of the road. I called him to ask him if he knew where his father was. The next thing I know, he was chasing me. For some reason he didn't want me to get here."

"Did you tell him that you were looking for me?"

"I told him that his father was a murderer. Then I told him that he was with my sister and I had to go and find her." I closed my eyes then dropped my head. My reaction must of have triggered something in Miles.

"Did you know John Jr.?"

I was very hesitant, but I responded. "Yes, it's a long story. I'll have to explain it to you at a later time."

"He and his father weren't that close. They're relationship was very strange."

"Speaking of fathers, who is our father?" We both burst into laughter. Miles notices an African American guy walking in the restaurant. He gets up and walks over to him. "Hello my name is Miles, Do you speak Spanish?" "Yes, what's up?" "I need a taxi to take me to the Paradise Resort." "No problem, I'll get you one."

"Hey Kyla, It's getting late. We've had enough news for one night. I have two beds in my hotel room. How about we get some rest, then we can discuss our travel plans tomorrow?"

"Sounds good to me." Miles leaves a twenty dollar bill on the table. Our taxi was waiting as we stepped out of the restaurant. The ride was completely silent. The two of us were exhausted. We both stared out of the window enjoying the beautiful sceneries. The Mariachi band was playing at a fiesta in front of the resort. When we arrived at the hotel room, I immediately jumped in the shower, put on my pajamas, and headed for the bed. Miles sat up in the recliner channel surfacing. We managed to tell our entire life stories within a couple of hours. I told him about Frankie, Sky, Taron and my cell mate Michelle. Miles began to feel very guilty of his life. I told him, that God has a plan for all of us and this was meant to turn out this way. I was so excited about Kevin. My heart went out to him. This man did a twenty-year bid for a crime that he didn't commit. Although, I was angry as hell with Judge, I still couldn't bring myself to hate him. I did not share my involvement with John Jr. with Miles at that moment. I don't know if I was embarrassed or just as guilty. I figured that I would wait until a later date to let him know about John Jr. The morning came very quickly. Miles made all of our travel arrangements. We got up early in the morning to catch our flight. We both slept the entire flight. When we arrived at the Philadelphia airport, reality smacked me right in the face. My fairy tale life was over. For once in my life, I felt like a queen. I had no worries and no pressure. I looked at life as a glass half full as opposed to half empty. I must say it felt good to be at peace. Now that I no longer have to run from John Jr., I can fight for Sky and continue to maintain my respectable, honest life. As we were riding home, we enjoyed the sound of Alicia Keys. "You never told me how you found out about me?"

"I'm a secret service agent."

"Stop kidding, I already knew that you work at Hockessin Hills. I think you're a nurse."

"Yes, I am a nurse. Once I found out that I was adopted, I started searching for my biological family. Suddenly, I staggered into a whole lot of other information."

"How much did you learn about our childhood before we were separated?"

"Not much, but I know a man that can tell you anything you need to know. Just let me know when you're ready to go and see him."

"Exactly how much time did he spend in prison?"

"Twenty years. Twenty long years for a crime he didn't commit."

"Who could we get in touch with to set him free? Now that we know he's innocent."

"He's already free. The funny thing is; he was free when he was in prison. This man is amazing. His spirit blows my mind. He left me a message that he was going to be released one day this week. He was paroled."

"That's great. Once I digest all this mess, I will give you a call so I can meet him."

"Sure, no problem."

We arrived at my apartment in no time. Miles helped me with my luggage, and gave me a big hug. "Thanks again for coming to get me. I'm really interested in getting to know you better. You seem to be pretty cool." "Yeah, you too." We both laughed. I couldn't wait to see Sky. Taron and Sherri were going on a marriage retreat, so I got the privilege to spend an entire week with Sky. She is so smart. She's all me. She even has a little street savvy for her age. "Momma, where did you get the name Sky from?" "Your uncle Frankie named you that. He's no longer with us."

"Where is he?"

"I believe he's in heaven. He died a few years ago." "

Why did he name me Sky?"

"Well…Frankie believed that the sky would be the limit for you. He wanted you to know that there is nothing, not one thing on this earth that you would not be able to accomplish."

"What does accomplish mean?"

"It means that with God baby, you can do any and everything. Uncle Frankie was a wise man and he knew that you were going to be a pretty, smart, and inquisitive little girl."

"I like Uncle Frankie." We both laughed. "Hey, you have another uncle that I want you to meet."

"Wow, I have another uncle."

"Yes, his name is uncle Miles. I'm calling him right now."

"Hello Miles how are you?"

"I'm okay, what's up?" "I was wondering if you could take me and Sky to see Kevin."

"Sure. How about tomorrow?"

"Just give me a time and we'll be ready."

"The earlier the better. How about I pick you up around 10:00 am?"

"We'll see you then." Sky and I had a great night. We watched movies and had a fun tea party. The morning came very quickly.

All of this was happening fast. One day I didn't have a family and no one to love. Today, I have a family; my daughter, brother, and a father. God was certainly being good to me. How often I have strayed away from my path and yet, He has never forsaken me. I pinched myself to make sure that I was not dreaming. I needed to speak to Ms. Neils. I knew she was the only one to make sense of all that was happening.

I arrived at Ms. Neils office approximately 8:00a.m. Immediately, I relayed the past several days of events to her. I was more than certain that she would understand. It was then that she relayed her own personal story to me. I was shocked to realize that she too spent time in prison and learning forgiveness put her back on track. She had fallen in love with a married man and became pregnant. He wanted her to abort the child and she refused. It was then that he turned on her. He had her framed for drug smuggling in Jamaica. Unfortunately, her daughter's first three years were separated from her own. Kinda, Lala, and Ness took the responsibility of raising the child until Ms. Neil's life was sorted out. Amazingly, we had some similar issues to deal with growing up. She too suffered from abandonment. Although she was beautiful and intelligent, her strength was in her ability to forgive and trust. She forgave her daughter's father and permits visitation. At this moment, I began to realize the strength in forgiveness. She taught me that harboring blame is the poison to the soul. At that moment, I ask that she pray with me.

I watched my time. I was anxious to meet Miles. It was a big day for me. Miles picked us up at 10:00a.m. sharp. "Who is this angel, oh let's see." Miles looks at his cell phone. "Hello God, I think you lost an angel" Sky starts to giggle. Miles picks her up and gives her a big hug. "Sky this is your uncle Miles."

"Mommy, he looks like you."

"You think so." Sky nods her head in agreement. Miles hands Sky a beautiful stuffed animal. When we arrived at the half way house, I noticed Kevin right away. He stood out like a sore thumb. It was like light was beaming around him. I then noticed that he was reading his bible. The three of us walked over to him.

"Kevin this is." Before Miles can finish his sentence, Kevin interrupts him."Kyla." His eyes began to tear up. He stretches out both of his arms towards me. He hugs me and begins to cry. He picked me up as if he was picking up a little baby. Miles stands there with a lump in his throat. Miles is trying to hold back his tears. Kevin then pulls Miles in our huddle. After holding us for a few seconds, "This pretty little princess must be your daughter."

"Yes. This is Sky."

"Well hello Sky, please to meet you. I'm Kevin." He gives Sky a big hug. The four of us walks over to a quiet area. Kevin stares at the three of us. "Kyla, you are so beautiful. I always thought you were going to be a princess, but I see I was wrong." He points to Sky, "Here's the princess and you're the queen."

"Thank you. Your hug feels just like I always thought it would. I waited twenty-three years for this feeling. I'm so glad to meet you." We talked for hours. Kevin gave us a history lesson on our past. It was painful, but it was needed. Then he switch subjects, "How have the two of you been, since your trip to Mexico?" Miles and I were startled. "How did you know about our trip to Mexico?"

"Judge Chapman came to see me."

Miles yells, "For what?"

"To ask for my forgiveness."

I interrupted him, "He has a lot of nerve. He is responsible for your twenty years in hell. You can persecute him and sue the whole judicial system for what he did."

"No, not exactly. The law prevents one from suing judges. But…If I truly wanted to I could go after the police department, city, and state. What would that solve? He asked for my forgiveness and that was good enough for me. So, I've forgiven him. How about if the two of you open your hearts and forgive him?"

"Man, how can you forgive him? He is the one who helped destroy our family."

"I can forgive him, because God has forgiven me. Besides I received the answer that I've been waiting for from God."

"You did! And what's that."

"God used Judge to let me know that I did not kill your mother. I've been waiting for that answer my entire life. Can you imagine the guilt I carried with me all of these years?"

"No we can't." I began to reenact the conversation that I had with Judge. I was drawn away from the conversation with Miles and Kevin. Then I heard Miles say, "Kevin you amaze me every time I see you. You are a hell of a man. I can't promise you that I'm going to forgive him." Kevin hands the both of us an envelope. "Where did you get this?" I couldn't believe the figures on this check when I saw it. "What is this for? This can't be for real. This check is for a million dollars."

"I know. Judge gave me these checks. They are from Robert Aston's estate."

"Who is Robert Aston?" "Apparently, Rob had given Judge some money in case his twins ever came to surface. He set up a trust fund for you guys. So I guess this is the money with interest. He gave him this money over twenty years ago." Miles blurts out, "His twins. I don't like the sound of it."

"Yes, the two of you. I told you that I was unsure about being your biological father. Let's be real, the two of you look nothing like me."

"It doesn't matter. You are my father and I don't want this guy's money." The both of us handed back the envelopes. It was very hard for me. I know God must be doing a serious transformation in my life. I just gave back a million dollars but I wanted Kevin to have it.

"You take it. You're the one who deserves it. You've suffered enough; they owe you. They don't owe us anything."

Kevin laughs and puts the envelopes on the table. "Don't be foolish. If the two of you want to do something that's worth more than money, then please forgive Judge. God will never forgive you if you don't learn how to forgive others when they violate and hurt you."

"Did Judge offer you any money? He thinks his money can solve everything."

"Yes he did. He offered me a lot of money."

"I hope you took it." Kevin gets up, gives all three of us a hug. His time is up. He grabs his bible and starts to walk away. As he was entering the next room, he turned around and said, "Hey Kyla, I'm saved and I love the

Lord, but I'm not crazy." Miles and I laughed. I picked up the envelopes and we all headed out the door. It was a quiet ride home.

"Miles, what do you think about what Kevin asked us?"

"I have a confession to make. I can't really pass judgement on Judge, because I wasn't always honest myself." I looked to the back of the car to make sure that Sky was asleep. "What are you talking about?"

"I had hidden motives myself. I was hired by John Jr. to seduce Judge into signing over some of his assets to me, so I can give them to John Jr." Miles looks at me with suspense. "So you knew John Jr. pretty well huh? How much was he paying you?"

"Nothing. I was in debt to him for another reason. But it's all over now and I feel guilty about everything. Judge treated me better than anyone in my past."

"Does Judge know that you were affiliated with John Jr.?"

"No. So I guess I'm no better than he is."

14

Judge is lying on the beach in front of his Villa. He is enjoying a glass of iced tea. Miles, Sky, and I walks up behind him. Miles hollers, "Hey old man, how about a game of scrabble?" Judge slowly turns around to face Miles. Before he could answer, I interjected, "He's not smart enough; he can't even beat me at Jeopardy." Judge drops a tear. He puts down his bible, gets up and embraces us. Complete joy was written all over his face.

Sky is running on the beach while Miles chases her. Judge grabs my hand and walks towards the water. Judge looks up at the sky and whispers, "Thank you Lord for answering my prayer." We had a great time in Mexico. Judge and Sky got along great. I was able to explain the entire situation to Judge concerning John Jr. He was shocked, but he forgave me; making it easier for me to forgive him. It was a joyous time for all of us.

When Sky and I arrived at my apartment, I was greeted by a priority letter. My heart felt like it dropped in my stomach when I saw this letter with no return address. I was hesitant about opening it. I said a little prayer then slowly removed the contents of the sealed envelope. I could not believe what I was reading.

My beloved Kyla,

I would first like to start by asking for your forgiveness. This is the hardest and by far not the smartest thing that I've ever had to do. I've been praying for weeks and I've been thinking about you for years. I ask God to let me reach out to you when you need it most and when it is the right time for the both of us. Well, as you read, you have already come to the realization that I'm alive. Not only am I'm alive, I'm also born again and I am a pastor. I have a beautiful wife and a set of twins by the name of Kyla and Taron. You can pick your chin up now. LOL. I've been drug free from the time I jumped out of that running car and I also hadn't performed any bisexual acts since then. God is so good and he's always had a plan for our lives. I knew that was the only way, God was going to be able to use us; we had to be separated. Separation was the only way I could clean my life up and to set you free. I was so dependent on you. You were my joy, strength, and love; you were my everything. There hasn't been a night or day that I didn't think about you or pray for you. I prayed that God gives both or us the power and strength that we needed to live not to survive. We are both survivors by nature. We needed to know how to depend on our Lord and Savior Jesus Christ. I've spoken to you plenty of nights through your cellmate Michelle. I explained my situation to her and I asked her to be my voice. I am so proud of you and I can't wait to see you. My children ask about you, Sky and Taron all of the time. They can't wait to see their auntie and I can't wait to hold my guardian angel. I love you Kyla. I thank you for everything and my heart yearns for your motherly love. Please forgive me and give me a call.

Luv Always,
Frankie

P.S.
I told you that it would be greater later!

Coming Soon

So What...
I'm Still Standing

A must read for all young ladies.

I would like to thank all of my readers for their support. I hope this novel was entertaining as well as inspiring. For anyone who feels lost, tired or fed up with life situations, please know that IT WILL GET GREATER LATER, and nothing last forever. I am a living testimony. I found my true peace when I dedicated my life to Christ and submitted to God's will. I invite you to try Him.

Love,
Yvonne

P.S. Did you read "Everybody Gets Tired"?

Order your copy of Yvonne's debut novel

Everybody *Gets* Tired

Richard Allen Projects, a world of drugs, violence, and poverty, fuses together three young girls in a bond of friendship and sisterhood. Kinda, Lala and Ness grow up in an environment believing that the three "B's beauty, booty, and brains, will bring them many rewards. A summer work program introduces them to Tay, an educated, beautiful "got it all together" sista that elects to take them under her wings and become their personal mentor, but, she selectively forgets to reveal to them "what she is really all about." As always, life takes many turns and the three friends shockingly must learn the truth about Tay while trying to cope with personal challenges of their own. The world of slick ballers and fast money, plunge their lives into confusion, desperation, and despair. Kinda, believing that the only thing a man is good for is money is forced to go on the run. Ness, believing that only one man can sexually please her, is fighting for her life. Lala, the voice of reasoning and the platform of stability for her friends, is left rendering support while maintaining emotional strength awaiting true love from her man.

Although young and still with many dreams, one by one they learn and realize that "Everybody Gets Tired". It will be their trails, tribulations, and ongoing hustles that make them come to terms with the street and their lives while learning that each mistake is a lesson and each lesson is a second chance at tomorrow due to God's grace and mercy.

QUICK ORDER FORM

Email orders: bridges2paradise.com

Postal orders: Bridges II Paradise
P.O. Box 67
Kirkwood, De 19708-0067

Name: ____

Address: ____

City: ___________________State ______Zip _________

Email address: ____________________________________

Shipping by air
U.S. $4.00 for first book; $2.00 for each additional product.

"Everybody Gets Tired" _________________

"It Gets Greater Later" ______________